Inklings Book 2014

Society of Young Inklings

The following young authors contributed their short stories and poems to this anthology.

Carmen Bechtel	Ellen Eckert	Alister Sharp
Mickayla Blake	Naomi Fuller	Cameron Shaw
Joseph Brentjens	Sankalpa Guitam	Kaya Shin-Sherman
Sophia Calegari	Benjamin Huang	Anya Singh
Suvali Chadha	Kevin Ma	Kevin Stovich
Joannah Cisneros	Amann Mahajan	Adrien Villanueva
Shaheen Cullen-Baratloo	Elle Marsyla	Natalie Wong
Kayla Davis	Lauren Massie	Emma Zhao
Ainsley Dillon	Sandhya Sundaram	

Grateful acknowledgement is made to the following mentors for contributing their editorial guidance and letters.

J.J. Austrian	Elizabeth Jellison	Helen Pyne
Andrew Avallone	Naomi Kinsman	Sarah Lyn Rogers
Melinda R. Cordell	Sara Kvols	Jessica Senn
Mandy Davis	Jennifer Mazi	Kelly Smith
Meridith Donahue	Polly McCann	Andrew Steeves
Frances Lee Hall	Erica McCuaig	Kristi Wright
Ann Jacobus	Jane O'Reilly	

Copyedited by: Sarah Lyn Rogers and Marilyn Hilton
Edited by: Naomi Kinsman

Printed in the USA
First Printing: July 2014
ISBN: 978-0-9910031-1-2

Table of Contents

Foreword

Who's to say authors have to wait to be published until they grow up? In the *Inklings Book 2014*, our sixth annual Inklings anthology, we are thrilled to feature short stories and poems by first-eighth grade authors representing five states and sixteen cities. Prepare to be amazed and inspired, and every once in a while, to laugh until your stomach aches.

After much deliberation, our editorial team chose these twenty-six winning stories and poems out of the many submitted for this year's writing contest. But, winning was just the beginning. Next, each young author worked one on one with an Inklings mentor through an editorial process that mirrors what the pros do. Our goal was to bring out the strengths of each piece and help these talented authors take their writing to the next level.

We've arranged the stories and poems to highlight the revision strategies used, and have included a letter from each mentor and an interview with each young author. This way, you can peek behind the curtain of the revision process and find excellent suggestions for your own work.

At Society of Young Inklings our goal is to inspire and encourage all authors, whether they've been writing for a very long time or are just starting on their writing journey. In these pages, we know you'll be inspired to dig deep and discover new ways to play with your writing. If this book leaves you hungry for more, check out our programs and resources at www.younginklings.org.

Showing Instead of Telling

Sara Kvols mentored Kevin Stovich through a revision focused on showing emotion through action in Kevin's story, "The Happiness Letter."

Dear Reader,

With descriptions playing a central role in Kevin Stovich's touching story about a weasel embarking on a journey to find the owner of a special letter, we focused on *showing* instead of *telling* in order to strengthen the way in which readers experience the emotion of the character's journey.

Showing a story is done by using details the reader can hear, taste, smell, see, and feel (sensory details). Through these, the reader experiences what the character is thinking and feeling. This is in contrast to *telling* the story, which simply details the events like a diary or summary. By engaging readers in the sensory experiences of "showing," the gap between reader and story closes.

One key to "showing" is action. Focus on the things that matter to your main character. Imagine how and why each action would impact your character, and then rewrite with the weight of the emotions your character might be feeling in that moment.

Another key is dialogue, which dives straight into the emotion and tension between characters. Unfocused or rambling dialogue can get the story off track, and a lack of dialogue can cause a disconnect between the reader and the characters. Find the perfect balance for your story by experimenting with when, why, and how the characters talk to each other.

A third key is emotion. Instead of naming the emotion (nervous, excited, bored), demonstrate the character's physical reaction. Continually ask yourself what your character is feeling and what that would look like. Then put those physical descriptions on the page!

One more important key to "showing" is description. Use strong nouns and verbs to describe what the

character hears, sees, tastes, touches, and feels, and try to do so through the eyes of the character. When describing characters, ask yourself what inner qualities a character has and how your description can reveal those qualities.

The adventure in *showing* your story is that it enables your readers to experience everything as if they are really there. Have fun with it—you can watch your story truly come to life!

Happy Revising!

Sara

Sara Kvols is a children's writer with a background in teaching and mentoring. She has an MFA in Writing for Children and Young Adults from Hamline University, and teaches communications, writing, and literature. She lives and writes from her home in northwest Iowa.

Kevin Stovich

Kevin is in second grade at Amber Campus Primary Plus Elementary School in San José, California. He likes reading, writing, piano, playing soccer and baseball, and building LEGOs. Kevin was born in Guatemala City, and loves to read and write action and adventure stories. Kevin has a pet guinea pig named Oreo, who sometimes sits on his shoulder.

Here are some of Kevin's thoughts on the writing and revision of "The Happiness Letter."

Why do you like writing?

Whatever story I write, I can tell what I am feeling. Instead of just showing my feelings in my own life, I can show them in my writing.

What was the hardest part of revision for you?

The hardest part was trying to come up with some new stuff to make the story even better. One of the biggest things was finding ways to put names in the story besides using name tags. I realized that names could be revealed in description or when a character had to ask the other characters.

How did the story change when you revised for *showing* instead of *telling*?

I thought it changed a lot. I changed how the character got from place to place, and I showed how the character felt emotionally instead of just saying how the character felt.

What did you learn from this process that you can use as you write your next story?

I'll use more descriptive detail, like instead of saying a character was depressed, I'll come up with new ways to show the feeling.

What advice do you have for other writers who might not be excited to dive into revision?

I think you should always try your best and also always remember that a suggestion is not something that is wrong—it's just something to work on to make the story better. Follow your dreams in trying to get your story edited. Keep trying and trying and even if your story doesn't win a contest like this or get published, keep trying and maybe it will get published.

The Happiness Letter

by Kevin Stovich

When we visited Chicago this past Christmas, a wonderful and mysterious thing happened. We saw the head of a brown and black weasel sticking up from a hole under the Picasso statue in the center of downtown. He was looking around and sniffing the air. Just then, he jumped into the air and ran straight for a piece of paper. He sniffed it. It smelled like honey, and the red ribbon tied perfectly around it smelled like peppermint. He saw that it was a letter and he tried to read what was written, but weasels can't read. Still, he thought it must be important.

"This is so nice and fancy," he thought, "that I should bring it to its owner," and he set off on a journey to find the owner.

The weasel thought for a moment and said to himself, "This is such a beautiful letter, maybe the owner likes beautiful music, too."

So the weasel went to the symphony concert. He listened and

listened, and thought the music was very beautiful. Just then, the weasel saw a little girl sitting with her parents. She had a really pretty dress with lots of sparkles, and she wore a pair of white sparkly gloves. On her dress was a label with her name. It was Avery.

"She has such a pretty dress," thought the weasel, "maybe this belongs to her."

So the weasel asked Avery for help, but she just said, "Shhhhhhhhh!"

Then Avery saw the letter. She untied the red ribbon and read the letter in the dim light of the concert lights. She smiled when she read the letter, gave the letter back to the weasel, and hugged her parents. The weasel looked at the letter, lowered his head and slowly walked out.

As soon as he got outside, the weasel heard a little boy say to his parents, "Mom, Dad, let's go to the Field Museum."

When they got into a taxi cab, the weasel jumped onto the back bumper. As soon as the weasel stepped foot into the Field Museum, he saw Sue, the gigantic T. rex, mouth open, pointy teeth, looking right at him. The weasel jumped, ran under a bench, and curled his tail into a little knot. A little girl saw him there, picked him up and started to pat his head. The little girl had blond hair that was very curly. She wore jeans and a blue top, and carried a bunch of books.

The little girl said to him, "Hi, I'm Lizzie. Don't be afraid. The T. rex isn't real – she's just a fossil."

The weasel did not know what a fossil was, and he tilted his head like he didn't know. He showed the little girl the letter. After she untied the perfectly tied ribbon and read the letter, Lizzie shot up with delight, hugged the weasel and ran to give her dad a hug. The weasel quickly tied the letter up, depressed. His whiskers drooped and his ears lay flat on his head as he started to leave the museum.

Just before he got out the door, the weasel smelled something delicious, so he followed the smell to the museum's coffee shop and bakery. The bakery was filled with bread right out of the oven and cookies. The weasel saw a girl picking out some bread. Her hair was brown, and she wore a white top and a sweater that was almost the same color as the letter's ribbon.

"Excuse me," said the weasel, "what's your name?"

"Stephanie," she replied.

The weasel showed her the letter and asked, "Is this your letter?"

"It's not mine," Stephanie said.

The weasel asked, "Can you read it anyway?"

She liked the pretty ribbon and after she opened it and read the letter, she burst out with joy and folded it up. She gave the letter back to the weasel and went to find her parents. The weasel looked at the letter, and he almost cried. He stomped out of the bakery and the museum. As he stood on the steps of the museum, he saw a sign for the "Winter Wonderland," written in lots of tiny snowflakes.

He said to himself, "I need a little happiness."

The weasel followed the signs to the end of Navy Pier and came to a big hall with a banner in big white letters that said "Winter Wonderland." The weasel snuck in and saw lots and lots and lots and lots and lots and lots and lots of jumpies, rides, and Christmas trees from different countries. His eyes popped open and his jaw dropped to the floor. Slowly he wandered from one jumpy to another, from the roller coaster in the center of the hall, to a giant blue zip-line, and he looked at Christmas trees from countries around the world.

The weasel went to the biggest jumpy of all. It was shaped like a polar bear and was as tall as a two-story building. Inside, there were penguins, slides and another polar bear. He stood in line behind a little boy who wore a gray shirt and a gray jacket and had brown hair. When they got to the front and took off their shoes, the weasel saw the name, "Noah," written in the little boy's shoe. The weasel showed Noah the letter.

After Noah read the letter, he said, "Thanks, but it's not mine," and gave it back.

The weasel looked at the letter and started to drag himself out the door.

"It's getting late," he thought. "Maybe I won't be able to find the owner of the letter."

As the weasel was walking back to his hole under the Picasso statue, he passed a butcher shop.

The owner saw him and said, "That weasel would make great sausage," and ran to try to catch him.

Just when he was going to kill the weasel, the owner's son, a boy who wore a black jacket and a red shirt and had black hair, saw him and the letter the weasel was holding. He begged his dad to stop hurting the weasel.

The weasel looked at the boy and saw his name tag.

He held up the letter and asked, "Ethan, is this yours?"

Ethan read the letter, gave it back to the weasel, and hugged his dad. The weasel walked out of the butcher shop, staring like a petrified zombie.

The weasel crossed the street and wandered through a playground when suddenly he got knocked down from behind by a boy who had black hair, black gloves and an orange jacket.

"Are you okay? You almost got hit by that swing" the boy said.

The weasel dusted himself off and stared at the boy. Then he handed him the letter.

"Is this yours?" he asked.

The boy looked at it and gave it back to the weasel.

"My name's Rod," he said. "Not mine."

The boy turned away and added, "Be careful!"

It was getting dark and the weasel was very tired as he said to himself, "I guess I'll never find the owner of the letter, so maybe I should just go home."

As the weasel was getting close to his home under the Picasso statue, he saw a little boy with brown hair, a blue shirt and an orange jacket looking around. The weasel thought the boy was lonely because he was all alone.

"What's your name?" he asked.

The boy answered, "Kevin."

"Why are you sad?" asked the weasel.

The boy answered, "Because I'm alone and I lost a letter from my grandma."

"Is this yours?" asked the weasel as he gave the boy the letter.

The boy broke out into a smile and thanked the weasel. Then he asked, "Do you want to come home with me?" The weasel thought it would be nice to live with a family, so he jumped into Kevin's arms.

When they got home, Kevin told his father all about the weasel and asked his dad to read his letter from grandma. It said, "It doesn't matter what you get. It just matters how much love you put into it."

THE END

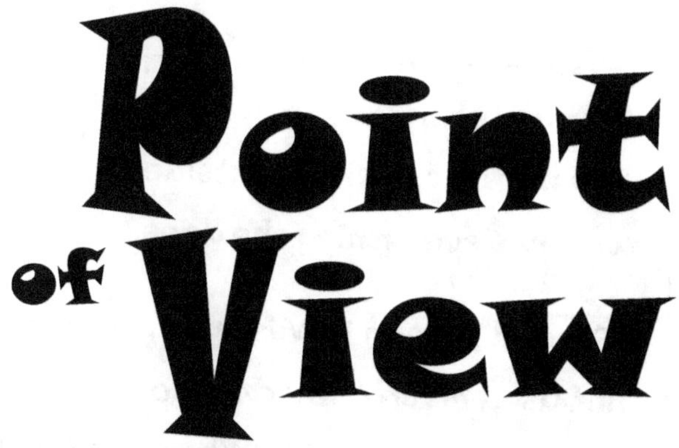

Melinda Cordell mentored Ainsley Dillon through a revision focused on point of view in Ainsley's story, "The Real Story of Humpty Dumpty."

Dear Reader,

In this revision, we looked at point of view.

What exactly is point of view? A simple way to think of it is to ask yourself as you read the story, "Who's holding the camera?"

In first person POV, "I" hold the camera. "I raced down the road, pursued by angry bunnies, so close that they kept biting the backs off my flip-flops." So the camera is in the main character's head, looking out through her eyes.

In third person POV, "he" or "she" holds the camera. "Maria raced down the road, pursued by angry bunnies that were so close they kept biting the backs off her flip-flops." The camera is outside the main character, but watches everything she does.

(Second person POV is "you," but it's a weird POV so it's not used much. "You race down the road, pursued by angry bunny rabbits. 'Who comes up with these crazy plots?' you ask yourself." The camera is in YOUR head here, even though it isn't. Anyway, it is weird.)

Then there's omniscient POV, where anything goes. So the main character gets the camera, but then somebody watching the main character holds the camera for a while, and then maybe they hand off the camera to God or to the narrator for a wide-angle shot of the world.

But the important thing to remember is that you have to be careful who you pass the camera to — especially if (spoiler alert) the main character falls and busts into a million pieces! So where does the camera go then?

A sudden switch of point of view is confusing. It's like you're walking along, looking at the pretty spring flowers — then suddenly you're a bird flying along looking at everything from thirty feet up. And then you're like

WHAT HAPPENED! WHERE AM I! WHAT'S GOING ON! and you crash into a tree.

That was a problem we came across in the story. When Humpty busted, nobody knew where the camera was. Fortunately that was easy to fix. Ainsley put a little space in the story after Humpty fell off the wall — added a couple of asterisks — and then she started the next paragraph with a little sentence to let the reader know where we were now. She also moved to omniscient POV, and then we were watching the scenes from outside the characters. Then when Humpty was fixed, he got the camera back again.

So when you're writing, keep an eye on that camera!

Happy Writing!

Melinda

Melinda R. Cordell used to be a horticulturist but now works as a proofreader. She has three hens who follow her around the yard. She is currently working on a book about the Civil War as well as 20 other projects.

Ainsley Dillon

Ainsley was born in Redding, Pennsylvania, on November 11th, 2003. She is now ten and attends Franklin Elementary in Liberty, Missouri. She is in fourth grade and is an only child with a kitten named Mittens. When Ainsley grows up, she wants to be a singer or a mechanical engineer.

Here are some of Ainsley's thoughts on the writing and revision of "The Real Story of Humpty Dumpty."

What changed in the story when you revised for point of view?

It changed because I had to figure out how to express an opinion that the Big Bad Wolf hated Humpty and I had to find a way to express that without changing the point of view.

What else did you change?

Actually not much – in my novel, the Big Bad Wolf is a good guy, and that's not something I can change.

What advice do you have for Inklings in writing a story?

My advice is, don't rush it, because you're going to have to go back and change the points that don't work. The longer you take to write your story, the shorter the revisions are going to be.

What are your favorite books?

The *Harry Potter* series and the *Divergent* series. I love every book I read because I get the good books from my mom.

Who do you like to share your stories with?

I like to share with the other girls who were writing with me and my friends. I try to read it the way I want it to be read and make it more interesting than when I actually wrote it.

The Real Story of Humpty Dumpty

by Ainsley Dillon

30

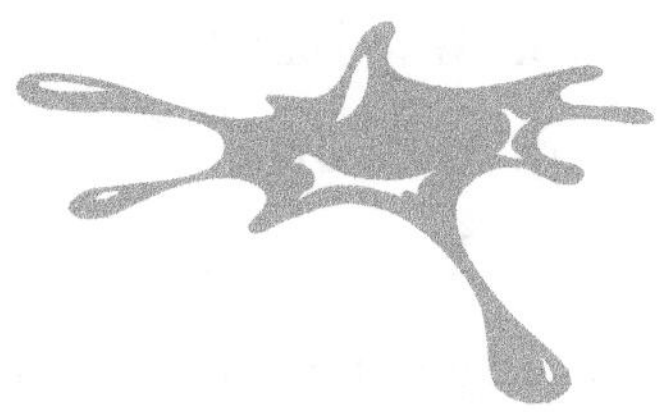

The forest thrived with the pitter patter of rabbit feet and the chirping of the birds. A fine fellow, I, Humpty Alexander Dumpty, held tightly on to my dragon Lucy's leash. The leash was torn and burned from when Lucy and I had spent countless hours playing fetch and tug o' war in our cramped backyard.

We frolicked down the path for a short time until we burst into the city. It's not really a city because it has the population of thirty-three. There's me, the Big Bad Wolf family of thirteen, the three pigs, and the king, age six, who has tantrums that can be heard throughout the kingdom. Then there are his five lazy men, and the wizard—the lonesome cat guy. There's my dragon Lucy, that wizard's five cats, and the three blind mice.

The Big Bad Wolf has always disliked me. He bullied me all throughout high school and almost pushed me to my cracking point in

Hatter High School football. He was even on my team! And now he's the manager of the Brick Making Factory (mine, rightfully).

Finally, Lucy and I were at the gates.

All of a sudden, the Big Bad Wolf's coach was in view. The windows were bursting with ten baby wolves. The eleventh, Mira Wolf, was curled up nicely on Mrs. Wolf's lap. Mira is the only sane child of her breed, if you ask me. And she has quite a good nose.

The coach stopped swiftly and Mr. Wolf came out with case number forty-nine clutched in his right hand. And there was yet another reason he disliked me: I knew his secret. Case number forty-nine was not yet for papers, but for scrambled eggs and bacon.

The thought makes me sick.

It's tough being an egg.

The coachmen asked where the Big Bad Wolf would like to be picked up.

"Here, at 5:30 pm, you brickhead! Do you think I want to go past the bloody village, or the Wizard's Tower, or the castle? No, I want you to pick me up here, so I can go home and go to bed!" the Big Bad Wolf shouted.

And that was that. Just like it has always been. Money put before generosity.

I sighed. Maybe one day things would go back to the way they should be. Then, Lucy and I walked up to the gates with the Big Bad Wolf at our heels. I opened up the employee pet cage and let Lucy in. Then I caught the door that Mr. Wolf rudely didn't leave open for me. I walked through the wooden doors and onto the brick floors.

I let it all come in at once. The hundred-year-old bricks'

musty smell hit me in the face with the old, dry clay. Across the room, I could see the three pigs snickering to themselves, and the third pig clutched the *Hatter Times*.

"What now?" I asked.

"Well, Humpty, it seems that the evil fifth-grade teacher has come to strike back. She's taken over the whole Hatter elementary and personally insulted the Boss today in the newspaper." They snickered even more.

Uh oh, this is not good, I thought. I swear that teacher is a jailbird.

"What'd she say?" I asked, a little frightened.

"Well, let me tell you," started the second pig. "I get to tell you because I was smart enough to build my house out of sticks. She said that he............hated his kids."

I started. "She can't report information that everybody knows and writes about. That's copyright."

Everybody knew that the only child that the Big Bad Wolf didn't dislike was Mira. I walked over and started pressing the fresh clay into the mold and sending it down the assembly line.

"Hello, scums. Hello, bugs beneath me!"

It was obvious who was speaking. I turned around to listen and with one swipe of my clumsy hands, in one motion, I knocked the now-dry clay onto the ground with a clash! Then Mr. Wolf jumped off of the marble ledge he was standing on and came so close to me I could smell his foul breath.

"Get your clumsy butt out of here, egg." He said *egg* like it was a bad taste in his mouth. "Go home and build a ten-foot-tall wall around it. STAT!!"

Of course I went, in fear of being cracked. Then I put a fifty-pound bag of clay into a wagon with a mold and set off towards home with Lucy, who had burned down the pet cage and walked behind me with her tongue hanging out.

When I got home, I put the mold down and started to work. Inhale, mold, exhale, put on wall.

I repeated this exhausting labor until I was done. The Big Bad Wolf came the next day to make sure my work was done. He came and looked astonished. I smiled.

"Walk on it. Make sure it's sturdy."

My smile disappeared. I climbed up on the ladder and carefully started to walk around the wall.

"Finally," whispered a soft voice.

I figured it out, but it was too late. I felt the claws skim my back, and I fell, and I fell.

"Put his remains in the crate," said King Richard, age six.

"Hey Richie," said Mr. Wolf nervously, through gritted teeth. "What are you doing?"

Lucy growled. "Shut it, Wolf. Or else I will personally grind up your teeth and you'll have to wear those false ones for life."

The Big Bad Wolf gulped and shut his mouth as instructed. Behind the edge of the wall, the Three Blind Mice giggled. They stopped when they got a devilish glare. Then the coach carrying Humpty was off to the Wizard's Tower.

When they got there, the smell of cats was overwhelming. The king knocked on the door and let himself in. One of the king's lazy men brought the remains up the stairs.

The wizard had put a spell on his brushes to groom all of his cats at once. Then he saw the king and his men and stopped chanting. The brushes dropped on the cats' heads. Several of them hissed.

"What brings the king here today?" the wizard asked calmly.

"I need you to fix someone."

"Oh, a broken heart. Those can be fixed in a heartbeat. Oh, get it? Ha!"

Nobody laughed at the wizard's joke. "No, no. Not quite like that. Bring in the Humpty." He went on: "This fellow's name is Humpty Alexander Dumpty. He is a fine fellow that is now the manager of the Brick Making Factory. Nobody has built a brick wall that was that tall that fast in years!" The king pleaded with his eyes.

"Yes, I can fix him."

Then the wizard started to chant:

Fix this fine fellow named Humpty

Whose name is no other than Dumpty

For he needs to live

Accept this gift that I give

Then the pieces of Humpty started to float and piece together.

I opened my eyes and stood up, wiggling my fingers and toes.

Then I saw the wizard, the king and…..Lucy! staring up at me with wistful eyes.

Then the wizard laughed. "For a second there, I thought that my magic didn't work!"

The king glared at him. The wizard stopped laughing.

"You're manager now and have been moved to a huge house with a huge backyard," said the king to me.

I couldn't believe it! Yeahhhhhh!!!!!!!!!! Then I ran outside to see a new house on the block. Then I ran to my new house and opened it. Then I went to one of the huge rooms and fell right to sleep.

The NEXT DAY

"I plead guilty for Mr. Wolf at attempt to murder," I said.
"I agree," the king said. "The End."

And what a happy ending it was.

THE END

Cultural Detail

ane O'Reilly mentored Emma Zhao through a revision focused on cultural detail in Emma's story, "The White Lace."

Dear Reader,

"The White Lace" is the heartfelt story of a little girl named Tikva who comes to America from Russia in 1936 and struggles to find her place in a new culture. The author, Emma Zhao, had already achieved this great story by the time I read it. She had also chosen a unique way to tell Tikva's story, a journal format, which not only allows her main character to express her secrets, but also illustrates how alone Tikva is in her new country.

Emma also knew her character well: Tikva never sacrifices who she is or what she believes in to make friends with Jessie and Jane. She knows right from wrong—even in a culture she is just beginning to understand. As readers, all we need by the end is a glimmer of hope that Tikva will survive in her new home, without her mother, which Emma delivers.

Because character and theme had been so deftly accomplished in "The White Lace," I suggested to Emma that she focus on the details, particularly cultural details that would illustrate differences between her old and new environments. I suggested that she look at pictures of immigrants in New York City in 1936, and that she imagine walking home from school in March. I also asked her what language the old man spoke. But the best question I asked Emma was, "What is your main character's name?" With that detail, in one single word, Emma told us a lot about her brave character. Tikva means "hope" in Hebrew.

As you revise your stories, use your five senses to add colors, sounds, tastes, smells and textures to your story. Imagine yourself as your character encountering things for the first time—every detail will help set the scene and drive the emotion. As I told Emma: Details will help your readers see, hear and feel the differences your main character experiences in her new world. Through these details, they will share in her confusion when she doesn't understand something and her

excitement when she does. If your character also finds something that reminds her of home, we will feel her joy, and maybe her homesickness, too.

Of course, you don't have to cross the ocean to encounter differences between people—even cultural differences. Different cultures can be as small as your friends' families or a new classroom. Any situation where you are exposed to a new way of doing things can be considered a cross-cultural experience. But remember, you don't have to look next door to find similarities among people. That is why, almost eighty years later, Tikva's challenges in "The White Lace" will still be felt by anyone who has ever had to move to a new city and make new friends.

Happy Writing,

Jane

Jane O'Reilly, who has mentored writers both young and old for years, holds an MFA in Writing for Children and Young Adults and is the recipient of a McKnight Fellowship in screenwriting. She loves unconventional formats but believes a good story, one that follows the basic elements of the craft, is why a book (or a movie) stays with you. She lives in Minneapolis where she is currently at work on yet another novel.

Emma Zhao

Emma is a third grader at Keys School in Palo Alto, California. Her favorite subject is art because she likes making things out of scraps—just like Tikva in her story. Emma also enjoys skiing and playing Uno and Monopoly with her family. When she is alone, she loves to read. Her favorite books are *Harry Potter* and *Warriors*.

Here are some of Emma's thoughts on the writing and revision of "The White Lace."

Why do you like to write?

I like to picture things.

How do you feel about revision?

My favorite part is deleting old work and putting in new work, but when I'm all done I feel like a massive boulder is gone from my head.

In one version of "The White Lace," you took out the part where Jessie and Jane tease Tikva about her accent. Why did you put it back?

I decided the most important thing I wanted [the readers] to know was that Tikva was Russian.

What's your favorite part in your story?

My favorite part is where I describe the lace like a woman dancing. I've always loved similes. But I don't like adding dialogue. If you asked me if I want to read a book with dialogue or similes, it would be one with similes.

What do you think is most important in a story?

A deep message.

The White Lace

by

Emma Zhao

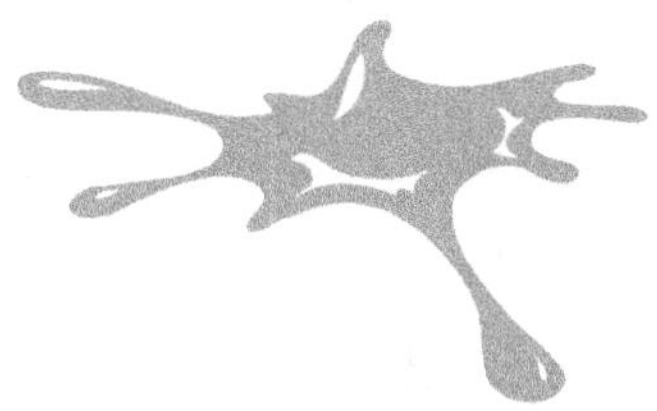

The Lower East Side
March 1, 1936

Dear Journal,

Every windy morning when I walk to school these days, I pass the tailor shop. Unlike the loud bustling streets outside our tenement, the shop is calm and quiet. The old man who lives there has white hair and a long scraggly beard. His eyes are pink and his eyelids are baggy, but the dresses and clothes he makes are fit for a queen. Whenever I peek into the window, there he is, sewing his beautiful dresses. What catches my eyes every time, though, is the lace on those dresses. The lace seems to glow and the strings weave around each other elegantly around and around like a lady in the ballroom. How I wish I could own one piece of white lace like that someday.

Tikva

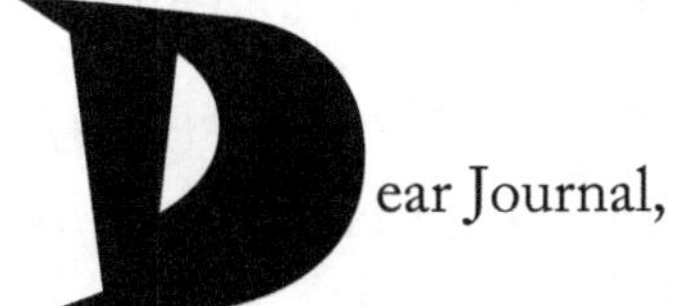

The Lower East Side

March 6, 1936

Dear Journal,

This morning, I passed the tenement buildings, the new Jewish market that opened two weeks ago, and walked by the tailor shop again. But when I peeked into the window, the old man was not there, so I took my chance and glanced at his workbench. A white shirt sat spread across the table. It had lace on the cuff and collar, and some buttons sat next to it, waiting to be sewn on.

As I turned around to leave, I noticed a piece of lace lying in the junk pile next to the shop. I picked it up. It was a little dirty and all cut up, but I think it's beautiful. I had hoped and prayed for months that I would find a piece of white lace and it had finally come true! I began to stuff it into my pocket when something caught my eye. Someone was watching me through the window. It was the old man. His eyes were stiff and there was no expression on his face. I quickly finished tucking the lace into my pocket and headed for home.

Tikva

The Lower East Side

March 10, 1936

Dear Journal,

Last night, I got out Mama's trunk from under the bed.

The cloth Mama had attached to the side was frizzled and dirty. The pink brim let me locate the lock easily shining in the starlight. Slipping my hand out of my pocket, I reached into my clothes and grasped the tiny key hanging from my neck. Unlocking the old rusty trunk, I found the lace I had put in and some of Mama's good luck buttons. I grabbed the cloth I had collected and started to sew. *So much for good luck*, I thought, remembering the night they had thrown Mama's limp body overboard into the big wide sea. But I added the buttons on anyways. Stitching the buttons on had taken hours of work: sewing them on, then taking them off and sewing them back on until they were perfect and in the right place. Midnight is how long the lace took me sewing some parts on, then cutting some off, then sewing some on and cutting some off. I had poked my finger a thousand times just to get the stitches right! But slowly by slowly the shirt started to form. Every little detail went into that shirt, and by 3:00 in the morning, my shirt was finished.

Tikva

The Lower East Side
March 11, 1936

Dear Journal,

This morning, Jessie and Jane teased me about my Russian accent. I felt really offended because I have been working hard on my English ever since I came here six months ago. They also said my clothes looked weird and ugly. I told them they better be quiet and leave me alone. They are so ruthless! Not only had I spent the whole night making this shirt, I even sewed on Mama's good luck buttons and the special white lace! I was not going to let anyone insult my shirt now!

Other days were like this, but this was the worst.

Tikva

The Lower East Side

March 17, 1936

Dear Journal,

This afternoon, I was going home when I saw the old man walking by. Suddenly, I heard screaming, an "oomph," and loud laughter. I turned my head to see Jessie and Jane running off, leaving the old man lying on the ground.

"Are you okay?" I asked the old man.

He didn't speak.

"Do you need help?" I asked again.

He nodded. I reached out to grab his arm and pulled him up slowly. Suddenly, he noticed my shirt. Pulling out eyeglasses from his pocket, he examined the stitches and felt the lace.

"Did your mother make this?" he asked in a gruff voice.

I shook my head.

"I made it myself." I replied. "My mother passed away on the journey here, but she taught me how to sew when I was little."

My throat clenched as I realized what I had just said. I closed my eyes and tried hard to fight back my tears.

"*Molodyets*," he said.

I smiled. That means "Well done" in Russian.

"*Spasibo*," I said, thanking him. "I got the idea from you."

"I know. I saw you the other day collecting the lace," he said. "Would you like to learn?"

"Can I?" I shouted, not believing my ears.

"Would you like to be my apprentice?"

Mama, now you can be proud of me. Because I finally found real hopes and dreams in this new country.

Tikva

Backstory

Jessica Senn mentored Lauren Massie through a revision focused on developing backstory for Lauren's story, "Paint a Picture."

Dear Reader,

When I first read Lauren Massie's story, "Paint a Picture," I was struck by her ability to capture landscapes through vivid descriptions and unique images. Her writing was poetic and flowed as rhythmically as the ocean she described. I wondered, though, about the main characters, Marcus and Janet. I didn't feel that I knew them very well, and their connection at the end lacked the impact I knew it could have. The story needed to flesh them out for the reader: to explain what made them tick, what they'd been through, and what they wanted in life. In short, it needed backstory.

Backstory refers to any actions or events that occur before a story begins. Backstory is important because it helps the reader understand who the characters are and how they became a particular way. After reading the first draft of "Paint a Picture," I wondered what was causing Marcus's pain. Had he lost a loved one? Was he lonely? I needed to know more about his past to understand his present.

Lauren did an excellent job answering my questions through a bit of backstory. During revision, she added a memory of Marcus losing his parents and being forced to live with his aunt and uncle as a child. Through this memory of feeling abandoned, I understood why Marcus might have trouble connecting with others and building long-lasting relationships. Lauren also incorporated some backstory for Janet, Marcus's love interest, which helped us understand why these two would be a good fit. To add layers to your writing with backstory, as Lauren did, you need to first get to know your characters on the deepest level, and then weave select pieces of information into the story in a graceful way. Neither of these tasks is easy!

As you get to know your characters, don't worry about what bits of information are going to make it into the final story. Pretend you are a biographer exploring every aspect of their lives. Draw a picture to figure out your character's appearance; make a timeline recording important life

events; describe a day with your character, from the moment he wakes up to the second he falls asleep; think about your character's fears, secrets, and dreams. Now ask yourself, what information does the reader need to know in order to make sense of your character's actions and emotions in the story you're writing?

There are several ways to gracefully introduce backstory into your writing. Remember, you don't need to give the reader all of your character's backstory at once: you want to sprinkle it throughout, like little puzzle pieces that eventually fit together to create a complex person. Lauren used a memory in the form of a short flashback to tell us about Marcus's childhood experience. In the present moment of the story, he sees marigolds and says, "Suddenly, I remembered my days as a child. How could I not? My parents' favorite flower was the marigold." Lauren then uses two short paragraphs to tell us about his parents' deaths and his feelings of betrayal. Flashbacks are often longer than this because they include whole scenes, complete with description, dialogue, and action, that take place in the past. Backstory can also come in a single, telling sentence, as when Janet narrates, "She said that I needed to get out more and maybe even meet

someone because I was working too hard on my novel."
This single sentence informs the reader that Janet is a
writer without much social life. A mix of succinct bits of
information, either through internal dialogue, memories,
or external dialogue, and slightly longer flashbacks, is an
effective way to mix in backstory.

Just like real people, your characters' pasts play an
essential part in making them unique human beings. The
challenge is making sure that rich backstory makes it from
your imagination to the printed page.

Happy Writing!

Jessi

Jessica Senn is a fiction writer and fifth-grade
teacher at the Phillips Brooks School in Menlo Park. She holds a BA
in English from Stanford University and an MFA in fiction writing
from San Jose State University. Her story "Christmas in the Desert" was
published in *Cicada*, and she is currently at work on her first
young adult novel.

Lauren Massie

Lauren is a sixth grader at Redwood Middle School. She plays competitive soccer and likes to go on camping trips with her family. When she grows up, she wants to play soccer on the USA National Team and write about her experience. Her favorite color is yellow because it is the happiest color and it reminds her of all the sunny things that happen in her everyday life.

Here are some of Lauren's thoughts on the writing and revision of "Paint a Picture."

How did you come up with the idea for "Paint a Picture"?

I have a really hard time thinking of what I want to write about, so I thought about it a lot, and I didn't think of anything. But then it was close to when the story was due, so I just started writing. It just came to me. As a family, we go camping a lot at a beach, and so I did that as the setting because one of my strengths is describing scenery. I decided to talk about that and a painter, and then I just kept typing.

What did revising for backstory add to "Paint a Picture"?

When I added the backstory, you could kind of connect with the characters more and you felt like you knew them more.

Did you learn anything new about your characters as you revised?

Yeah, I think so. I knew the characters, but incorporating that into my story was a little hard. As I kept trying to incorporate more into my story, I figured out more things about what I should add or tell about them, wondering, "What's their favorite color?" and if there's a good place to put that into the story.

In your mind, did you already know that Marcus's parents died in a car crash? Did you already think of him as an orphan before you began revising?

Yes, I had already thought of that. I didn't realize some things, though, like at the beginning it said, "Painting a picture is a difficult task because you're trying to make the person looking at the painting think about what they really know," but the story was really more about feelings, so I changed it to "what they really feel."

What was the hardest thing about revision?

The hardest thing was incorporating information. I had a really hard time with that. I knew the characters really well, and I knew where to put in backstory, but it was hard to decide how much. I also tried to put it throughout the story so it wasn't all just in one place, everything about the character. I had to sprinkle in little details.

Have you ever revised a piece of writing so extensively before? How was this experience different from your typical revision process?

Yeah, I revise for school, for reports and stuff. I have my dad read it, and he makes a couple notes. Last time I had a report, he highlighted everything that was confusing and added notes, so that was really helpful.

What advice would you give other writers about revision?

You shouldn't think too hard. Like, it should just come to you and it shouldn't be stressful.

Are you working on a new story?

Mostly I just write my ideas down for when I'm older, when I know all of the writing tools that will make my stories better.

Paint a Picture

by Lauren Massie

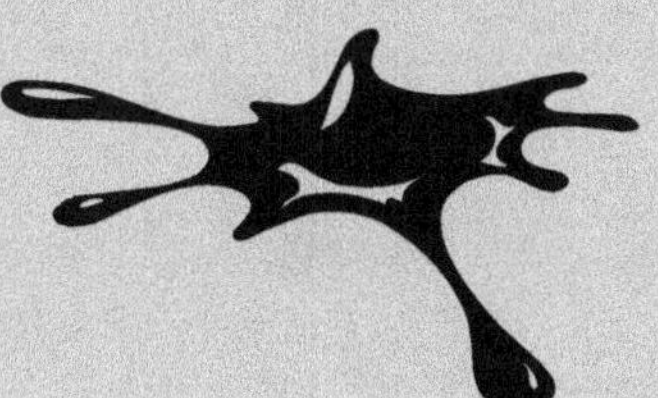

Life as we know it is really, really difficult, but it is even harder when you're all alone. Painting a picture is a difficult task because you're trying to make the person looking at the painting think about what they really feel. You might just learn something or find out what you're missing in life. Maybe you'll find your way to true happiness.

I walked outside with a canvas, paintbrushes, and some paint, shutting the door after I stepped out of my tiny cottage along the cliff's edge. The fog came in, resting on the hill looking over the sea as it moved in a continuous motion forward and then back again. Thoughts went in and out of my mind as I continued meandering along the path towards the sea. As I got closer to the beach, I could feel the ocean breeze and smell the salt lurking within the clear blue water, one could tell you were almost there, yet I had no intention of going to the beach to run along the waves today. I was going to paint a masterpiece to send to the gallery in the city. There was going to be an art gala soon and I certainly did not want to miss it, for I considered myself one of the best artists in town. I chuckled as I sat in the long grass along the side of the cliff and looked out into the sea.

The breeze tickled my hairy chin as I looked for something to paint, preferably gorgeous scenery. It didn't take long to find something to paint. The marigolds were dancing on their stems as they spun around their fellow flowers in unison, feeling the sun's golden rays and looking up at it soaking in the warmth and desire for more. Hummingbirds were singing a calming tune that the yellow blooms danced to. Soon they began rotating their wings, gloriously dancing to their song. You see, an artist always looks for something heartfelt to paint. The inspiration has to feel real, as real as suffering, exposing one's true feelings. An artist cannot hide behind a wall of aloofness.

My hopes and dreams are my canvas. They allow me to enjoy myself and release the stress hanging on so tightly. Find your passion. It will allow you to release your fears. Everyone has them. Release your aches and pains because there's no point of playing joyfully when all you can think about is the pain that is taking you down with it, or that's what I say.

Suddenly, I remembered my days as a child. How could I not? My parents' favorite flower was the marigold. My parents came to all my baseball games and they would be the loudest ones on the stands. The redness on my face would reveal my insecurity, but I also felt a warm glow inside my heart. A cold soreness hit me as I remembered how happy I used to be, before the accident.

The memory of the car crash flooded my mind, and I couldn't help but feel sorrow.

I remembered walking up to my crazy Aunt Beth's apartment. My grandma was holding my hand as we walked up the steps. The feeling of hatred fell over me. How could my grandma give me away? It wasn't my fault my parents were gone, so even if I reminded her of them, we should help each other through it, right?

I looked up at the sun and felt the rays take over my body. Then I looked down at the blank canvas and began. My days of misery and anger were over. I've come too far to let the past reenter my life. Besides, I love living here. Where I feel like I belong.

I started with the thick strokes of brown mixed with a little green for the majestic mountains in the distance. They always stood high above the clouds where they were isolated from the world below. I could always count on them.

Next, I decided to use a thinner brush to portray the rushing waves that crash over again and again, turning from an icy blue to a snowy white in the process the moon was instructing. In the painting, you can see the little indications of the dolphins jumping and the birds gathering around in midair, getting ready for feeding time right off the great Pacific on the coast of California. Days like these are ones to remember with someone and you'd say to them, "Oh, don't you remember that day, that perfect day where the sun was shining high in the sky, the waves were crashing down like tigers growling at their prey, and the aroma of the sea salt drifting with in the refreshing breeze?" Those would be great days.

After I finished painting the waves thoroughly, I thought of turning the painting upside down to show a different way to view the coasts. All the beach paintings are pretty much the same, and I wanted mine to be different. When I turned the painting upside down I thought of how could anyone not like a new perspective—my perspective of a beach painting.

So, I turned the canvas upside down and started painting the green meadow on the cliff side where I was sitting. This new section was going to be the bottom part of the painting. With a little hint of yellow and brown I made the meadows full of marigolds and trees where you could see little hummingbirds flying above the yellow blooms, humming a happy tune. It made one feel like they were there sitting beside you, smelling the precious whiff of the ocean and feeling the sun shine so brightly.

Finally, I had finished my masterpiece and it was ready to send to the gala that would be portraying it soon enough. Since it was a little past noon already, I decided to go back to my lonely cottage and make myself a homemade lunch that would contain a little Caesar salad, a misty Sprite, and some saucy spaghetti.

It was easy for a man like me to make a meal like this. I had no cooking skills whatsoever, and this was as easy as it comes. I longed for a wife that could cook for me, someone who thought about life in creative way and saw things differently like me. I sighed and took the painting into the attic. It needed a frame, and I knew the perfect one. It was golden with mint green carvings that looked like dolphins.

The next day, I walked over to the gallery where Ken, the gallery owner, was working this peaceful afternoon. He was taking other artists' paintings into his work room, so I met him in his path and gave him my piece of art. Ken smiled as he took the painting and put it beside the others.

"Aha, Mr. Kinkle, you have truly made this gallery proud. We love showing your work, and this one is magnificent."

"I was sitting up on the cliff side just yesterday morning and started painting the beautiful scene when I decided to do something different and turn half the painting upside down to give the guests at the gala a new perspective of the beach."

"Well, it sure gives me a new perspective!" Ken said to Marcus.

"By the little tingling inside my stomach I know that it must be very special."

"Goodbye, Marcus Kinkle, and see you tonight at the gala. It is going to be spectacular."

Ken thought to himself, Boy, I really like him. Marcus reminds me of myself. He even looks like a younger me with his dark black hair covering his blue eyes over that pale skin he has. No wonder he has a sense of humor like me. He's always so energetic when it comes to imagination, I guess that's what it is like to be young these days. I can't wait to see how much someone will pay for this piece. I'd better get to work then if this gala is going to be a success.

Actually, I'll take a break, grab a coffee and enjoy this work of art.

I see the ocean swirling onto the sandy beach. The waves are spinning in circles of blue and white where the dolphins are jumping and the birds are feasting on the juicy, or shall I say scaly, fish. In the background, the bulky mountains are rising high above the hills, and look at those paintbrush strokes. They make it seem like the mountains are flat and curvy, making their way to a world beyond ours.

The painting has been turned upside down now, where I can see the marigolds hidden in those strands of green grass that are flowing in the wind, moving side to side with the ocean breeze. The hummingbirds are flying above the meadows, probably singing their happy tunes. I can hear them now.

That Marcus is one incredible artist, maybe even the best in town. The gala is going to be one to remember. Mr. Kinkle might even meet a girl that suits him.

Staring at the gallery across the street, I heard Monica yelling my name, "Janet!"

Monica was meeting me at the gala. It was her way of getting me out of the house. She said that I needed to get out more and maybe even meet someone because I was working too hard on my novel. She was always trying to help, but sometimes she couldn't see life the same way I did.

The music was playing loudly and I could see her waving to me. I tried to hide, but it was too late. I was so nervous. My dress was gorgeous and I knew it, but somehow I still felt very uncomfortable. It was as gold as the sun, with white lace trim. When I twirled, it looked like the sun's rays were jumping off me and turning some people's frowns upside down. I hoped I looked like I was ready to have a good time. Maybe I don't get out enough.

After we entered the gallery, I started walking towards the paintings and stopped when I thought I saw a surprising variation of colors. Or maybe it was not just full of color;

maybe it was something else. It was simply beautiful. I thought I knew the painting, but just when I felt I knew what it was, it caused me to feel something in a different way. The painting was very confusing.

Different colors vibrated throughout the picture. I wasn't sure what I was looking at until it hit me. It was a cliff view looking down at the ocean and the hills surrounding the sea. That sure took a lot of imagination to paint something as sophisticated as this.

"Do you like it?" Someone close by interrupted my thoughts.

"I think it's marvelous, maybe even one of the best paintings I've ever seen, yet I don't understand what the artist is trying to portray. Do you know, umm, Marcus Kinkle?"

"Actually, I am Marcus."

"Oh, well, you look quite stunning tonight," I said over the music, quickly, not to be rude.

"Thank you, but I prefer to be called handsome," Marcus added, laughing a little at his own joke.

"Sorry, I don't really get out a lot," I replied.

"Neither do I," he answered. "What is your name?" he quickly asked.

"My name is Janet, or that's what my friends call me."

"Maybe I'll see you again," he said as I moved on to the next painting.

I knew I would see him again as I turned around and his smile lit up his face. I think I just met my prince charming!

68

Elaboration

Meridith Donahue mentored Ellen Eckert through a revision focused on elaboration in Ellen's story, "Cinder Athlete."

Dear Reader,

Ellen Eckert's story, "Cinder Athlete," puts a modern-day twist on the classic Cinderella tale. Ellen's retelling of the fairytale was already rich with sensory detail and lively writing; however, we decided to work on elaboration to slow down some scenes that needed more detail.

Elaboration can help slow your story's pace down when you've gone too quickly. Sometimes you need to get your ideas on the page, so you accidentally leave out important details or information because you were in a hurry when you wrote.

You can check your own story to see if it could benefit from elaboration by reading it through and looking for places where your story needs more information. Are there scenes that need to be a little longer? Have you skipped describing something important? If you want, ask someone you trust, such as a parent or a teacher, to read over your story.

Mark the places in your story that you think need elaboration. If you're having trouble getting started, close your eyes and picture one of those scenes. This is a game called Frozen Moments that we sometimes play in Inklings classes. Act out or think through the scene as your main character. Slow down and take in the details of the scene. What's there that your character didn't notice before? Is it important? How does your character feel right now? Make sure to go through your character's five senses, too. Think about what happens in your scene and why it's important to your story. Is there something your character should be doing that she isn't? What does your character need to do next? Finally, how can you add all of that to your story?

These probably seem like a lot of questions! Take them

one at a time, and have fun with this exercise. If you do,
you'll discover so much more about your story and be
glad you tried it.

Happy Writing,

Meridith

Meridith Donahue has an MFA
in Writing for Children and Young Adults from Hamline University.
She loves being an Inklings instructor and is hard at work revising her
young adult novel.

Ellen Eckert

Ellen is an animal lover. She has three dogs and one cat. She wants to be an author/vet when she grows up. She is nine years old and she attends Roosevelt Elementary school. She lives in Faribault, Minnesota. She loves babies. In fact, she has three baby sisters. Her favorite subject in school is, of course, writing.

Here are some of Ellen's thoughts on the writing and revision of "Cinder Athlete."

When did you start writing?

When I first learned to write, maybe at five-and-a-half or six. I started writing little mini-stories. I kept one that I wrote in kindergarten. It's only three sentences long, but it was the most I had ever written at that time. I wrote another copy of it in second grade and it's three pages now.

I always wanted a desk, but I had to share a room with my sister. My mom found a house and I get my own room

with my own desk. I have lots of privacy for writing. I don't want people to see my writing until it's finished.

What was your favorite part of revision?

Probably saying, "Did I really leave that out? Really?" I like making my story better. In almost all of my stories, I describe my characters, and so I can't believe that I forgot to describe Cinder Athlete.

What advice do you have for other Inklings who don't like to revise?

Just keep trying. Just know that people are going to read this and you don't want any parts missing, so you need to be persistent. Keep trying, keep doing this until you're fully satisfied. When people ask you to revise, they're not trying to be mean. They're actually helping you. Add to your story. I had some mistakes in my story even when I thought it was perfect.

Describe how you got your idea for this story.

My little sister really likes fantasy. If you read a nonfiction story to her, she'll fall asleep, but magical stories keep her awake. Fairy tales are her favorite genre. I asked her what I should write a story about, and she said, "Cinderella." The next day, my teacher said we needed to write a fractured fairy tale. I asked a classmate what two words should go together and he said, "Michael Jordan." I thought about sports then. My brother is really sarcastic, so I asked him for two words, and he said, "Athlete!” One of my sight words for school was “cinder,” and I put “cinder” and “athlete” together.

Do you like to read? What are your favorite books?

My favorite author is Andrew Clements. He is my most beloved friend. I’ve read all the books in our classroom library. *Frindle* is my favorite out of all of them.

What do you do if you get stuck?

If I’m typing, I’ll usually stop and try to write by hand. If I can’t do that, I read something classic, like *Harriet the Spy*. I always read that and I’m like, “Hey, I have an idea!” I think *Little House on the Prairie* and *Harry Potter* are good because they have cool details. If I’m still stuck, I sleep on it. I’ll go around and ask people for more words that go with what they said before. If my mom said, “magic key,” she might say, “magic key hole,” and I’ll usually get an idea.

Cinder Athlete

by Ellen Eckert

76

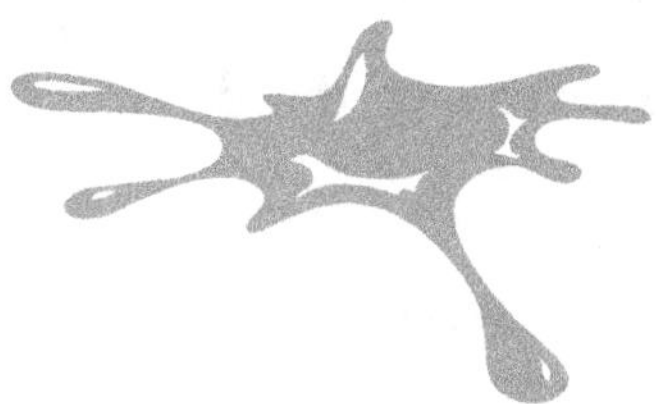

rack, Crack, Crack went the fire. It was thunder storming outside. Lightning touched the ground, not too far away. Then, thunder rumbled and shook the house. But inside the house, they were all safe and warm. The fire was roaring, but not louder than the storm.

"Grandma please, please, please, tell me a nice story," begged a little girl named MaryAnn. She was scared.

"Okay. But you have to promise to be quiet. The baby is sleeping," said MaryAnn's grandma. "It all started long ago in a far off land…"

Squish, Squish, Squish went Cinder Athlete's mop. It was disgusting how sour-smelling the mop water smelt after so much mopping. Cinder Athlete was dressed in torn, dirty sweatpants, and a way-too-big brown and dirty T-shirt. Her mother made her wear those clothes. Her mother was jealous of Cinder Athlete's facial beauty, so she dressed her in the worst possible clothes while she dressed herself in the fancy gowns and clean white tights and perfect high heels.

When there was company, she locked Cinder Athlete in her room upstairs so whoever was at the door would focus on her beauty, not her beautiful daughter's.

"Time to get your sorry butt out of here," said the Cougars' coach. Cinder Athlete's favorite team was the Cougars. That's why she mopped for that team instead of the Rodents. Yuck!

Ignoring the rude comment, Cinder Athlete politely said, "May I stay and watch them play?"

"NOOOOOOOOO! You're just the ugliest distraction I've ever seen! Now GOOOOOOOOOO!!!" said the mean coach.

Cinder Athlete hurriedly wrung out her mop and put her mop and bucket away in the storage room. Then she bolted towards the door and ran home. The run home was lonely and bitterly cold. She wondered if she would get some dinner. She wondered if anybody would ever accept her for who she was. But mostly, she just wondered.

That very night, her mom wouldn't give her any dinner. These were the exact words that came out of her mouth: "No dinner for you. You are thirty seconds too late!"

So, Cinder Athlete went to her very wet room, jumped into her very shabby bed, to cover up with her blanket (that she was still cold under), and went to sleep.

In the morning, Cinder Athlete woke up bright and early, because she wanted to get an early start for an early finish so her jealous mother would finally give her at least a little bit of leftovers for her supper.

She threw on the clothes she had on yesterday afternoon. Then, she crept quietly out the door for fear of waking up her mom. Next, she ran to the Cougars' practice gym. When she walked in, the lazy, no-good coach was sitting on a wooden chair, cleaning her favorite red whistle. She was a Neat Freak. Cinder Athlete went to get her broom quietly, and quickly. Then she got straight to mopping the floor. It was just starting to get light out.

Cinder Athlete had just started to mop the floor when she noticed a poster taped to the wall. She glanced at the coach. Yep. Still didn't notice me, Cinder Athlete thought. She took a step closer.

It said, "Free pick-up basketball game! All you need to bring is your own tennis shoes and your own ball! Have fun and make new friends! Tomorrow night from 6:00 to 8:30."

I wish I could go, thought Cinder Athlete. Wait a minute… Maybe I can go!

That night you'd think that all of Cinder Athlete's attention would be on the fact that her mother finally gave her some burnt, leftover fish heads. (Ewww! she still thought.) But instead, all of her attention was on the basketball game that she was going to tonight.

After she finally choked down those gross burnt fish heads, she wiped her face with the back of her hand, because she was in such a hurry that she didn't have time find a napkin. She hurried upstairs to her wet room. She pulled open one of the damp floorboards and reached her hand into the dark, small space and pulled out a pair of sparkly red sneakers.

This was her secret hiding place. The reason she had to hide anything that looked good and fashionable in that spot was because her mother would definitely not let her wear anything that only had a smudge of dirt on it. In reality, it had to be torn in many places for Cinder Athlete to even think about wearing it.

Then, she pulled out a clean, barely used, bright orange basketball. She had never used it. Well, she only dribbled it in her room sometimes. And she was glad she didn't use it that much, so she didn't have to pump it full of air. It really made this night way easier than it would have been. Finally, she pulled her hair up with a matching red ponytail holder. Then she climbed down the ivy vine that grew up the side of the house. She knew that it would come in handy. Then, she jumped off the bottom of the vine when she was close to the ground. Next, she started to break into a fast jog down the dirt road.

A feeling of guilt and excitement built up in her. She had to be home by 8:00 because that's when her mom came into her room to check on her. The wind tugged at her sweatshirt. Almost like it wanted to drag her home. But she pushed on. By now, Cinder Athlete could see the faint glow coming from the windows of the gym and jazzy music flowed into her ears. She also recognized the gross smell of sticky sweat. She slipped into the gym and quickly pulled up her sweatshirt so nobody would recognize her. Not that anybody would, for Cinder Athlete had no friends.

But still, she didn't want Coach to recognize her and say, "Hey, you're just the mop girl. Now scram!"

So she strolled in, trying to be as casual as can be. Nobody turned to watch her. Good. Nobody really knew she came in. So nobody would tell on her.

Trying to be quiet, she listened to the sounds in the gym.

She heard happy chit-chat and some happy people yelling and shouting. Then she thought, I'm never happy. I'm always miserable. Nobody likes me. I shouldn't be here where everybody is happy. But, ignoring her feelings, she started dribbling her basketball and shot a hoop. In no time at all, she was playing like mad.

She was just about to shoot her ninth hoop when she felt a hand on her shoulder. She was scared that it might be Coach coming to fire her because she was not allowed to come to a pick-up basketball game where everybody was allowed to play. But she turned around anyway. It was just a young girl. A feeling of relief swept over her.

"Do you want to shoot some hoops with me?" said the girl.

She smelt like the beach and her voice was shaky, almost scared, as if she was afraid Cinder Athlete would be mad at her for asking.

"Sure," said Cinder Athlete, excited that somebody actually wanted to play with her.

A look of relief took over her face. The girl was wearing baggy boy shorts and a jersey that said "Cougars 21" on it. She was part of Cinder Athlete's favorite team. They chit-chatted happily and pretty soon they were best friends. Cinder Athlete learned that the girl was the same age as her and that she went to the private school. Cinder Athlete told the girl that she didn't go to any school because the most her mom spent on her was a couple of dimes at the most. For once, Cinder Athlete felt like she belonged.

After they shot at least fifty hoops, they took a water break. Cinder Athlete asked the girl what her name was and the girl said that her name was Briana. Then, Cinder Athlete glanced at her watch. It read 7:54! Without a word, Cinder Athlete bolted out the door. As she was running down the gym stairs, she tripped and one of her tennis shoes fell off! She couldn't stop now, so she kept running. She felt as if she were racing against the wind. When it was 7:59, she finally climbed up the ivy vine and hopped into her bed. Two seconds after she got into bed and covered herself with the blanket so her nasty mother wouldn't see her wearing good clothes for once, her mother turned the squeaky doorknob to Cinder Athlete's room.

Right when she came in, she said, "Go to bed, you nasty creature!"

Ignoring the rude comment, Cinder Athlete sarcastically said to her mother, "Good night to you too, Mother."

With a toss of her curls, her nasty mother walked out the door. Cinder Athlete tried counting sheep, but before she could count to five, she was fast asleep from all the excitement.

Cinder Athlete was woken up by a loud knock on the door. She rushed downstairs, hoping it was for her. She had thrown her soggy robe so nobody could see her basketball clothes. When she got to the bottom of the stairs, she stopped. Nobody was ever at the door for her, and barely anybody knew her name. So, she turned to go back up stairs.

Just then, the door opened. Cinder Athlete smelt the beach. It couldn't be Briana… Could it?

"I want to speak to a young girl." It was Briana's lovely voice.

Cinder Athlete went back downstairs. She smiled when she saw Briana. Briana recognized Cinder Athlete's smile and instantly tried the shoe on her. It was a perfect fit! Cinder Athlete heard some noisy whispers coming from outside her kitchen door. It sounded like a mob of people.

"What is going on here?" asked her mother.

"What's happening here is this girl right here is the best basketball player that I have ever seen and she's going to join my team!" That was Briana all right. Then, with big, begging eyes, she asked Cinder Athlete, "Will you?"

Then Cinder Athlete shouted, "YESSSSSSS!!!!!!!!!!!!!!!!!!!!!!!!!"

The next week was the Cougars Championship game. In the last five seconds, Cinder Athlete made the winning goal against the evil Rodents! And, her mother started giving her good clothes and full meals because Cinder Athlete was becoming famous, and her mom wanted to be famous just like her. She even let her go to the private school with Briana and they lived happily ever after!

MaryAnn's grandma smiled when she saw that MaryAnn was asleep on the couch. She crept silently up the stairs. She went into her room, opened a loose floorboard, took out a basketball and smiled.

THE END

Choosing a Central Story

Erica McCuaig mentored Anya Singh through a revision focused on choosing a central story in Anya's story, "Anna's Animals."

Dear Reader,

Just as people are shaped by their origins, so are stories. A heavily planned and researched story might have a completely different personality than one born of a burst of inspiration. For stories, just as with people, it takes all kinds.

Any writer knows that different writing processes have different advantages and pitfalls, though. Planning a story well allows for more intricate twists, gives a story structure, and enables an author to use techniques like foreshadowing most effectively. However, it can be difficult and labor-intensive. Free-writing gives a writer the freedom to follow their imagination wherever it leads. The danger of this type of writing, though, is that it can lead to stories that lack focus or continuity. This is a situation in which mindful editing and revision can be vital.

Anya began "Anna's Animals" with a setting in mind, and then just started writing. The story evolved from there and took a number of turns as her inspiration struck. In editing this story, Anya focused on bringing together the different events and settings she'd created to form one unified story. She needed to choose the characters and events that she felt were most central, and then decide which elements of the story to incorporate and which to eliminate.

Choosing a central story, as this process could be called, helps the author clarify the message and decide what story is really being told. Scenes, characters, or descriptions might need to be deleted, edited, or added. An author might even find that some characters or pieces of the story can be taken out and developed into new, separate stories. The possibilities there are

endless!

Whichever process an author chooses to use in creating a story, it is important that the author is able to effectively convey his/her message to the reader. This can be accomplished by planning out a story out ahead of time, using certain techniques during the writing process, or clarifying things in the editing process. Which specific tools or tactics an author uses are less important than the end result of a clear, effective story.

I hope you enjoy reading "Anna's Animals," and that you feel how Anya's love of both nature and animals is expressed through her tale of a girl and her dog.

Happy Reading!

Erica

Erica McCuaig is a lifelong resident of California. After graduating with a BA in psychology in 2008, she spent time working in the field of social services before turning her full attention to writing and teaching. She is currently an instructor with the Society of Young Inklings, and is working on her sixth collection of poetry.

Anya Singh

Anya was born in New York and lived there until she was 5. She then moved to the Bay Area with her family. She enjoys playing the piano, writing, playing tennis, and playing handball. She also likes spending time with her family and having fun with her brother. Anya has been interested in writing from a very young age. She has always had a strong imagination, and she brings her love of animals and magic to her stories.

Here are some of Anya's thoughts on the writing and revision of "Anna's Animals."

How do you feel about this story - "Anna's Animals"?

I feel good. I feel happy because I finished it and it was chosen. It feels like an accomplishment.

Why do you enjoy writing?

I like it because I'm the one that gets to write it. I like it because I can make my own stories up.

Where do you like to write?

I like to write at home at the kitchen table. Sometimes I write other places, but that's my favorite.

How do you come up with your ideas?

Well, I thought of the main character first and then I picked where the story would happen. I chose the sea because I really like it. I like animals too, and I used these ones because they're my favorite animals.

Do you like to read? Who are your favorite authors?

I like to read books about dogs. I also like books about history.

Who do you share your ideas with?

I share them with my mom. I just want my mom to hear my ideas and give me advice.

Are you writing a new story now?

Not yet. I'm working on some poems right now in my secret journal. It has a key.

What other activities/hobbies do you have besides writing?

I like playing piano and I like playing tennis. I like handball at recess. I like playing with my friends too.

What advice do you have for other young writers?

Just think of something in your life or something you like, and then write about that.

90

Anna's Animals

by Anya Singh

92

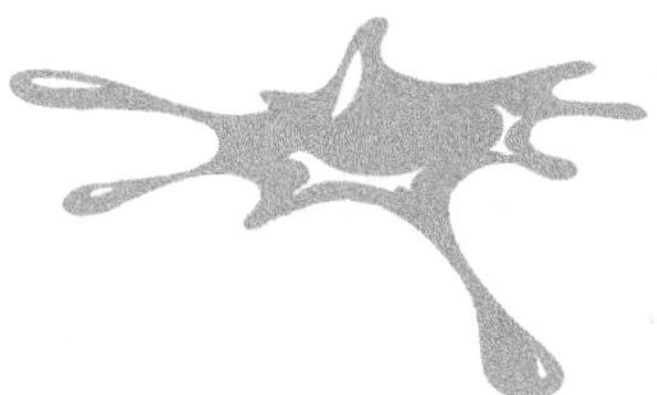

Once there was a blue sea that had many fish. There were many fish colors like blue, orange, and many others. There was also a baby shark with her mother. There were three dolphins. They all lived together like a pack. The sea was very rocky. The shore was very sandy with many beautiful seashells. There were a lot of sand castles. It was hot and sunny and seagulls were flying around the beach.

Near the beach, Anna lived in a cottage with her mother and father. A long time ago, they lived in an apartment, but Anna didn't like it so they moved. Anna liked spending her time with her dog, parrots and dolphins. She went to the beach every day and those days were the best.

Anna had blue eyes and brown hair. She loved to play with her two parrots and her one dog, called Cleo. She loved to watch and feed the parrots. She loved to play with her dog and chase her and feed her.

But most of all, she loved to go to the beach with them. She swam and made beautiful sand castles. She loved to watch the dolphins when they went up and down. There were dolphins everywhere.

Cleo also loved going to the beach. She loved to dig in the sand and chase dolphins. She loved to run with Anna in the shallow water. They splashed together and Anna threw a toy in the water for Cleo to get. Cleo loved to talk with dolphins. Cleo barked and dolphins made sounds back.

One rainy day in the sea, the dolphins were happily swimming. Suddenly, the weather changed and dark clouds came. The dolphins swam very far and lost track of their home. They came to a dark and scary cave. They went further and further through the tunnel and cave. Soon they came out but didn't recognize where they were. They knew they were lost and they were very scared. They continued forward.

In the meantime, the first one to wake up was Cleo. That was because Anna forgot to put her inside. Cleo went to the beach and dove in the sea and started swimming. The dolphins called for help and she heard them. She successfully led them home. Then, Anna saw what had happened with the dolphins. Anna was very happy that Cleo was able to save the dolphins even though she was pregnant. She was Hero Cleo! Anna rewarded her with a treat and went in the backyard to play with her. They played tug-of-war and ball and everybody was very happy.

It was early morning and Anna saw that Cleo would have a puppy really soon. Anna thought, *This will be a great year for her and her animals.* Anna needed her mom to drive Cleo to the vet. In the car, she was constantly petting the dog and telling her to be brave. Cleo looked scared but she knew she was in good hands.

They went to the front counter to speak with the receptionist. She told them to wait a little, as the doctor was seeing some other dogs. Soon, room 54 was available and Cleo, Anna, and Anna's mom went inside.

After a couple of minutes, the vet came in and said, "Hi, my name is Mrs. Dryn. Oh well, well, we will see new puppies really soon."

Anna could not wait. Her mom could not wait. But Cleo was still scared.

Mrs. Dryn said, "Follow me," and Anna's little family moved to a special room where Cleo would bring her new puppy to the world.

Anna and her mom left the dog and stepped outside. They had to wait in the waiting room until the vet called them. But Anna was tired and she excitedly fell asleep. Her mom woke her up telling her that Cleo had given birth. They went inside the special room and saw the most beautiful golden puppy in the whole wide world.

Cleo was resting and Anna had to give a hug to the newborn puppy. She took him in her arms and the little golden puppy licked her on her nose. Anna knew she was in love again. The first time was with Cleo and now with her newborn puppy. She was so happy. She decided to call him Goldie.

On the way home, she stopped at the pet store to pick up some pet treats and a big dog bed for Cleo's new family. When they went home, everyone was tired and Cleo took a nap in her new bed. Anna gently kissed Cleo and Goldie. Then she went to her room and snuggled with blankets to sleep too. It became dark and quiet.

Suddenly, she heard howling and she jumped out of the bed. It was Cleo. She was scared as she was not able to find her golden puppy. She was very upset. Anna turned the light on and saw Goldie under the table. She picked him up and brought him to Cleo. As she was looking at Cleo and her new golden beautiful puppy, she knew many adventures would follow them.

THE END

Finding the Heart of the Story

Helen Pyne mentored Sandhya Sundaram through a revision focused on finding the heart of the story in Sandhya's story, "The Imbroglio."

Dear Reader,

I was dazzled by Sandhya Sundaram's suspenseful story and hooked the moment I read her first two lines. Drawing inspiration from Greek mythology, and epic Indian tales, "The Imbroglio" is a beautiful tapestry of action, suspense, strong characters and sweeping emotions. I particularly liked the way the story was told through multiple perspectives. But because the plot was complex and there was a lot of background information that readers needed to know, Sandhya's challenge was to find a way to weave together meaningfully the lives and histories of her three, different point-of-view characters as she built to the climax.

Consequently, our primary revision strategy was to focus on finding the heart of her story. With so many balls in the air, Sandhya had to figure out what information was most important to include, what motivated the people in her story to do what they did, and how the relationships her characters had with each other helped to shape and transform them. Here are a few examples of questions Sandhya tackled. Why did Norah feel so driven to save the world? How was it that Maeve remained good, while Vesper grew selfish and evil? Why does Adonai decide to plunge back into the danger he'd just escaped in order to help Norah? Once Sandhya answered these questions, everything fell into place, and she knew what to do to revise.

While Sandhya's initial conclusion tied up all the plot elements of her story, I felt it did not fully resolve her characters' emotional journeys. In the original ending, orphaned hero, Adonai, and his pet monkey were left adrift; the reader did not know where they went or what they did after the story ended. But in the revised

ending, Norah asks her new friends, Adonai and Babu, to come live with her (and Maeve and Vesper). This gesture felt very right to both of us, and in this way, Sandhya was able to craft a more logical, satisfying and heartwarming conclusion to her story. When authors focus on finding the emotional heart of their stories, they are often able to get new insights into their characters and plot.

Happy Writing,

Helen

Helen Pyne has an MFA in Creative Writing for Children & Young Adults from Vermont College of Fine Arts and works as a freelance writer, editor and creative writing instructor. Past jobs including working at Seventeen Magazine and as a children's book editor at Doubleday and Cloverdale Press, a book packager. She's published two books in a mystery series for young teens and currently writes for *Appleseeds Magazine*.

Sandhya Sundaram

Sandhya is a sixth grader at Redwood Middle School in Saratoga. Her hobbies include volleyball, singing and playing the piano. Someday she hopes to be a software engineer and founder of the largest company in the world. She lives with her parents and nine-year-old sister.

Here are some of Sandhya's thoughts on the writing and revision of "The Imbroglio."

What was the revision process like for you? What changed in your story when you revised by focusing on finding the heart of your story?

> I thought that the revision process was really helpful. When you write a story, there are often many problems that you don't notice yourself, and I thought it helped a lot to have a mentor. When I shifted my main focus to "finding the heart of my story," it helped me focus better and not stray off or change the theme. It helped me carry out a main idea throughout the story.

Your story is told from the point of view of three different characters. What do you like best about writing in multiple points of view? What do you find most challenging about it?

I feel that when a story is told in multiple points of view, it gives the reader different characters to sympathize with and understand deeper what others think. When I read books written in different perspectives, I get attached to all the important characters, and that is a paramount part of the story. The hard part was arranging all the parts of different characters in the correct order so that it would make sense to the reader.

When did you first start writing fiction?

Since about first grade. That was when I took off and began writing random stories in an old composition book. They weren't the best, but I really used to enjoy writing science fiction, fantasy, and humorous stories, that I would also use to entertain my younger sister.

The choices your characters make are at the heart of your story. Was it hard to figure out what motivated them to do the things they did?

Some parts were especially hard. Some decisions were momentous, and crucial to the story, but thinking why a character would want to make those decisions was hard.

How did you come up with the idea for this story?

Honestly, I didn't use any planning or organizer. I just let my thoughts flow and wrote nonstop for hours at a time. As I wrote, I added new characters, plot twists and other elements. That's the way that I write best.

Many people dream of having special powers. Did you give Norah the kind of powers you wish you had?

I brainstormed all powers that a character could have. Being able to create illusions and imitate sounds is a really cool power to have. I love to imitate voices and sounds myself, and many of Norah's traits come from or relate to myself.

The Imbroglio

by Sandhya Sundaram

104

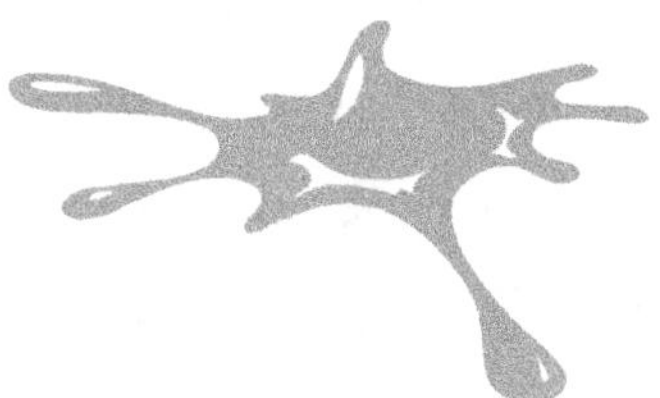

When Norah Clifton was born, her parents looked at her with disgust. They took her home, put her in a breadbasket, and disposed of her in a gutter.

Later in the night, it rained. The innocent infant and the basket floated down the gutter, collecting the murky rain. Norah drifted all night and fell asleep to the rhythm of the pouring rain. Most little ones would have wailed and been petrified, but that wasn't the case for Norah Clifton. Norah had no knowledge of this, but she really wasn't normal. She had the extremely rare ability to create illusions; one of its side effects was her ability to imitate any sound she heard.

At this point in the story, it is necessary that I give you some history. Ten years prior to Norah's birth, there lived two sorcerer twins, Maeve and Vesper Reverie. These two siblings were the only ones who held the secrets to keeping the world at peace. Using their magic, they managed the world and ruled it well. They were very close to each other, but their strong relationship was torn apart when they broke out in a bitter quarrel. Vesper and Maeve's parents had died in a tragic accident, and the two faulted each other on their deaths. They argued all day and night. Finally, they decided that the only solution was to separate for life and never speak again. So Maeve and Vesper parted and went their own ways, hiding from everyone. But they were so vital to civilization that the world became a land of chaos, disputes, and war.

This continued even after Norah Clifton's birth. A prophecy stated that a girl, with the help of two friends, would save the Earth's inhabitants from the disaster that would inevitably follow. That was Earth's only hope.

The next morning, an old lady found baby Norah in her basket, lying in the gutter. She took pity on the child, kept her, and raised her as her own. Years passed and Norah grew up to be a beautiful young teenager, but the tension in the world did not stop.

The time has come for me to introduce two new characters to the story. Adonai, a nine-year-old boy, was a thief. He lived with a tribe in the rainforest and was an expert on artifice. On his side, he carried a leather pouch, which was filled with various concoctions, potions, and powders that could affect a person in many different ways. Adonai was frustrated. One moment he had been happily swinging about in the trees of the jungle with his pet monkey Babu. Then he was grabbed by some men, knocked out of his senses, and his memories of the last few hours were erased. Now he was handcuffed inside a dark prison that smelled of rotten cheese and stale bread. He sat on a stone ledge, with Babu by his side. He didn't understand. Why would some random men imprison him for no reason? From the moment he was placed in the dirty prison cell, Adonai had been thinking of every possible method of escape. Babu smiled at Adonai. He probably had no clue what was going on. Neither did Adonai. Neither did anyone else in the world, except Vesper Reverie.

"Mother Gretchen?" called Norah.

"Mmmmm?" The old lady smiled as she combed back Norah's long silky hair.

"Why isn't the world peaceful as it used to be? I love your stories of the old days when everyone smiled and the world was happy. I wish this would change," she said.

"We're just waiting for the one girl who, according to the prophecy, will make things right," Gretchen said, placing her bony hands on Norah's shoulders. "I'll get going. I have things to attend to."

If only I could be that girl, thought Norah, and her mind immediately began investigating possibilities. From the moment she'd heard the story of Vesper and Maeve, Norah had wanted to be the girl to change the world. She would use her power of illusions even though Mother Gretchen had forbidden her from just that. Norah's mind wandered off to a memory. She and her best friend, Celeste, had fooled their school teacher into thinking that there was a pig in the classroom. The teacher got furious, and Norah and Celeste were suspended. Gretchen immediately banned Norah from exercising her powers.

Never mind that, Norah thought. She was determined even though she knew that many had tried, but failed to restore peace.

Suddenly, there was a knock at the door. Gretchen rushed into her room, and peered out the window, where a messenger and his horse were waiting patiently.

Who would I get a message from?

Questions flooded her mind as she went outside to get the letter.

"Yeah, I'm Gretchen. I'll take this message. Thank you. Have a nice day." Gretchen talked in an abrupt manner.

Desperate to know what the message was about, she ripped up the envelope, and began to unfold a scroll of parchment. The address was familiar; Gretchen knew of the wealthy merchant who lived at the famous Vortex Palace. She furiously read the letter, which was scribbled with a felt pen.

Dear Gretchen, I'm sure you know who I am, but keep reading anyway. I have a master plan. Meet me at my palace tomorrow at 2:00 pm (address is on the envelope) to discuss things. Sincerely, Vesper Reverie.

Vesper Reverie is the merchant! she thought.

"Oh no! What is going on? What does the evil Vesper want?" The poor old woman fainted.

Later, after she recovered, Gretchen went to Norah's room.

"Norah, dear? Are you in there?" she said as she knocked on Norah's door.

"Oh yes, Mother Gretchen. Come in," said Norah.

"I have to meet someone—for business. It's quite a ways away, and I must leave this evening. Can you manage by yourself?" Gretchen said tentatively.

Norah's mind was on fire. This was the perfect opportunity for her to run away and save the world.

"Yes, Mother Gretchen. What sort of business is it,

anyway?" Norah asked curiously.

"It's nothing. Just with an old friend of mine." Norah noticed that Mother Gretchen hesitated when she said "friend."

Later that evening, Mother Gretchen left in a horse-drawn carriage. Norah got to work the moment she could. As she searched the house for her sweater, her eyes alighted on a piece of paper with notes scribbled by Mother Gretchen: *Vortex Palace - meet Vesper.*

Vesper? Reverie? Vortex Palace! I thought Cliff Jones, the wealthy merchant, lived there! Oh no! What does Vesper want with Mother Gretchen?

Along with the address were brief directions.

I can't let Mother Gretchen be alone with Vesper!

Norah left home, and made for the thick rainforest, which she would have to cross before reaching the palace. She crossed cities, used her powers to steal a motorbike, and rode to the jungle. Hours went by and Norah finally arrived. The journey had been long and beads of sweat glistened on her face. It was approaching evening and darkness would surely get in the way. The forest looked massive and impenetrable. Just looking at it made her shiver. Norah hid her stolen motorbike beneath a bush and began to swing on the long vines of the lush rainforest towards the palace.

Vesper Reverie sat waiting patiently on the porch of Vortex Palace. Oh, there she comes. Finally! Vesper's lips curved outward into a smile. Gretchen arrived in her carriage. She frowned at Vesper.

"How nice to see you again, Maeve, or is it Gretchen - isn't that the name you take on now? It's been ages."

"Yes, Vesper. Now what is it you called me here for?" Maeve's lips trembled as she spoke each word. Vesper looked vastly different from how she remembered him. His eyes were a piercing blue and his hair was combed back and gelled. Maeve tugged on her hair - it was a wig, which she took off. Her real hair hung down in silver wisps.

"Ah yes. I've been thinking." Vesper took a moment and looked at Maeve. "You look so different, Maeve. So old," he said.

"Yes. Now get on with it. I don't have all day. I have a daughter eagerly waiting for me at home."

"Okay. I have a fabulous plan. When you and I ruled peacefully together and controlled the world fairly, things didn't work out. We had an argument that took things downhill. This chaos will stop if we rule over the Earth once again. Except this time we make all people our slaves. Every single person, except the two of us," he concluded.

Maeve froze. "Does every person include my daughter?"

"Yes of cours—" Vesper started.

"No! No Vesper! This is not happening. Not on my life! This is evil, Vesper. Evil. To everyone! Why can't we rule as we did before? Where everyone was… happy," Maeve finished. Tears streamed down her cheeks. The tension was rising, and the furious Vesper was ready to explode.

Adonai knew how to escape! How stupid of me not to think of this before! he thought. The guards who guarded day and night usually got tired when it was second shift. The lazy fellows always fell asleep. If Adonai could sneak past them, then he might have a chance. But everything had to be well timed with no delays.

He remembered the old days, in the jungle, when he lived with his mother and father in a rainforest. For hundreds of years, Adonai's tribe had lived in there. One day, a merchant deforested a large part of the rainforest, to build a palace in the center. He ordered that all the tribespeople were to be killed. At the time, Adonai had befriended a monkey, Akachi. Akachi helped Adonai escape from being killed, but Adonai watched in vain as his family and only friends were slaughtered. Akachi gave birth to a baby monkey, which Adonai took care of when Akachi went out to get food. On one such occasion, Akachi was spotted, and shot dead by the merchant. Adonai wept for days, wondering what to do. Adonai kept and trained the helpless little monkey, and named him Babu. Since then, Adonai and Babu stole for a living, and lived alone in the rainforest.

Adonai's biggest regret had always been that he never helped his tribe or saved anyone. He'd always wanted his revenge on the evil merchant, but he didn't know the way to his palace, and had never been there. Adonai shook himself out of his memories, remembering the escape that was to come. He whistled for Babu and the cute monkey hopped onto his shoulder. Adonai took a sleeping remedy from the leather pouch he'd hidden in his clothing and handed it to Babu to put in the guards' water bottles. Babu came back, smiling at the marvelous work he had done.

Sunset approached and Adonai and Babu were ready.

"Okay, Babu. You know the drill."

Babu stealthily crept out of the cell. He found a sleeping guard and he stole his prison keys without the faintest sound. Adonai waited patiently for a few moments and went to meet Babu at the entrance. It was a majestic iron bolted gate, with intricate coiled copper designs. Adonai took a moment to take in the breathtaking view. Below him, he could see the tops of trees, vines, and lush, tall grass. It looked vaguely familiar. By the time he got to the entrance, Babu had already opened the doors for him. They made a run for it. After sprinting far enough out of the prison, Adonai peered back. The prison was a tiny corner of a huge palace bearing a bold sign that read, "Vortex Palace."

Just as Vesper was about to blow up and scream furiously at Maeve, two guards interrupted and walked in. "Sir Vesper. Sorry to interrupt, but we uh uh… We kinda have a problem here," said one of the men.

"Well for gods sake tell me!" Vesper was getting increasingly irritable every second. He was like a bomb. The beeps would sound faster and faster before the final explosion. "The prisoner - that young boy - escaped with his monkey! Well, what are you waiting for, you nitwits! GO AFTER HIM. NOW!"

Adonai heard loud thuds. He looked behind, and saw a bunch of prison guards chasing him. RUN!! Babu got the message. They ran as fast as they could through the jungle, and Adonai realized that they were escaping the palace of the evil merchant.

Norah was almost there. She could see the grand palace. She was exhausted so she rested on a low branch of a banyan tree. At a distance she spotted a boy and what looked like a monkey being chased by two tall men. The poor boy looked helpless. As he ran past, Norah grabbed his arm and with all her strength pulled him onto the banyan tree. She then used her power of illusion to make the guards think they could still see the boy by mimicking his screams. One moment the boy was ahead of them, the next moment he was gone. The guards were dumbfounded.

"What's going on?" Norah asked the boy.

"Shhh!" he whispered back. The guards circled around, looking for any signs of Adonai. The boy motioned for Norah to follow him and they managed to creep away from the banyan tree unnoticed.

"What happened to the boy?" one of the guards asked.

"No idea. Why does Vesper need him anyway? I don't think it should matter," said another.

"Vesper believed that this boy came from the tribe that lived here before Vesper's palace was built. With this boy alive, Vesper will not be able to carry out his "Grand Plan" altogether because people from the Ahaju tribe possess rare magic, which could be dangerous to Vesper. I wonder what that plan is. He never tells us anything, yet we have to work for him!" the first guard replied. With more muttering, they marched back to the palace.

"Wow, that really is Vesper's palace!" Norah exclaimed.

"That's Vesper's palace? I thought it was the merchant; the evil one," said the boy at the same time.

"I thought so too, but apparently, he changed his identity. Oh yes! I am Norah," said Norah, as she held out her hand.

"Adonai," he said, as he took her hand. "And this is my pet monkey Babu," he said, as Babu showed Norah a toothy monkey grin.

"Can you explain what happened?" Norah asked, curiously.

So Adonai told Norah of his capture and his subsequent escape. He also told her of his tribal background.

"That thing you did there, fooling the guards. That was really cool. How'd you do that? And also tell me your story," said Adonai. And then Norah told Adonai about her ability and how she ran away in search of Vesper and Maeve. She told him that she might need some help in her mission. Adonai agreed to help Norah, and get his revenge on Vesper.

"Okay. Let's hurry. We're running short on time," said Norah.

"I know the way to Vesper's palace. Follow me," said Adonai. Norah followed Adonai through the vines of the jungle.

"But how are we supposed to get in?" asked Norah when they reached the palace.

"Oh. Here's the part, where having a monkey is extremely useful. Babu!" Adonai whistled for Babu and whispered into his ear. The clever monkey climbed up the palace walls, hopped into an open window, crawled to the front door and opened it for Norah and Adonai. Norah used her powers to make the three of them invisible to everyone who walked by. They climbed up the long spiral staircase until they reached a large room. They waited outside the door, watching a waiter go in, bearing a pot of tea. The three followed the waiter inside and spied Vesper Reverie sitting on a large throne. Norah looked around and spotted Mother Gretchen, imprisoned within a glass cage.

Making herself visible, Norah screamed, "Mother Gretchen!"

Vesper smirked "Hah! Mother Gretchen! You mean Maeve."

"No...Wait… It can't be. You've got the wrong person," said Norah.

"You tell your daughter yourself, Maeve!" said Vesper.

"Sorry, Norah, he's right" said Maeve. Norah was too stunned to move. Mother Gretchen was really Maeve in disguise all along?

Knowing that it wouldn't help, Norah tugged at the bars of Mother Gretchen's cage, crying loudly while she did so.

As this conversation went along, Norah's companions were getting busy. Babu scanned the room for keys to the cage, finding them dangling from one of the desks. Snatching them, he bounded across the room and unlocked Maeve's cage.

Adonai meanwhile was busy in his own way. He rummaged through his leather pouch of herb-based remedies, and looked for a suitable one. He scanned the room. It was dark and full of stone and glass statues, which Vesper was known to avidly collect. Adonai desperately looked for anything he could use. Oh there! The waiter's tray. That's perfect! Adonai slid under the table and slipped over to the waiter's tray. As a former thief, stealth was his practiced art. He grabbed a cup of tea, pulled out a powder from inside his belt and slipped it in. This would put Vesper in a lifelong trance. Members of the Ahaju tribe carried this extremely rare powder their entire life. They could use it just once. This was his time.

The waiter, who was busy sweeping the room, hadn't noticed anything. He now came back to serve the tea. "Vesper, sir. Your tea is ready." Adonai watched Vesper's stiff hands bring the cup to his lips. He drank deeply.

Vesper's servants were terrified of their master. They were trapped. Every day they yearned for their escape, but all were too afraid to take action.

As soon as Vesper drank, his eyes softened. "Winston," he said to the waiter. "You have my permission to leave Vortex Palace. But before you go, tell all the others that they can leave as well. You are dismissed." Vesper's words stunned everyone in the room. Winston left.

At first, Adonai had no idea what was going on. What had the trance powder done? Adonai then remembered. The powder could either ruin a person or change a person's perspective.

But Vesper wasn't finished. "Maeve. I'm so sorry. I shouldn't have even suggested that cruel idea. I want to rule again. With you. I want everyone to be happy."

Now, Norah and Maeve were speechless. Questioningly, Norah looked at Adonai, who mouthed, "I'll explain later."

Two days had passed since Vesper changed. The news that Vesper and Maeve were back was celebrated worldwide. Adonai explained what he and Babu had done. Then came the highly anticipated coronation day of Vesper and Maeve. They were crowned with flowers and then the ceremonies began. As the end of the day neared, people began to leave, but Norah saw Adonai and Babu sitting sadly in the corner of the balcony of the new Reverie Palace.

"What happened, Adonai. Why are you so sad?" Norah asked.

"Babu and I have no place to go, now that the Ahaju people are gone. I don't know what to do," he replied.

"Well, you can come stay with me, Vesper, and Mother Gretchen-sorry, Mother Maeve. I'm still getting used to the change. Anyway, I'm sure they would love to have you."

"Really?" Adonai's face instantly brightened.

Maeve and Vesper accepted Adonai and Babu with open arms. The little monkey was exuberant. The return of Vesper and Maeve was celebrated worldwide. Wars ended. But what really mattered was one thing - everyone was happy.

Internal & External Dialogue

Kristi Wright mentored Joannah Cisneros through a revision focused on internal and external dialogue in Joannah's story, "Slaying the Dragon."

Dear Reader,

With Joannah Cisneros' fast-paced and witty story about a young girl fighting real and imagined dragons, we decided to focus on internal and external dialogue to bring the reader an even greater understanding of the main character's motivation.

Both internal dialogue (a character's unspoken thoughts) and external dialogue (what characters say out loud) can be used to bring clarity to stories, either by revealing something important about a character, or revealing something important about the plot.

Here's one strategy for deciding whether you need more dialogue, whether internal or external, in your story and then where to insert it. Reread your story and see if you are left with any big questions about why a character did, said or thought something. If you are too close to your story to be able to see the questions, ask a parent, teacher or friend to read your story and tell you their questions. If it feels scary asking someone for so much input, ask them to limit themselves to their top two or three questions. You don't have to answer every question that someone has about your story, but these are excellent opportunities for dialogue.

Next, look through your story for spots where dialogue might be inserted without slowing down the excitement. One of the best places to add internal dialogue is either right before or after external dialogue. Alternatively, you could just add more external dialogue to bring clarity to the scene. Another place where either internal or external dialogue can be added is near action.

When deciding whether to have a character say something out loud or whether to have her think it, often it depends on how sensitive the thought is. For example, if it is something that someone would feel

embarrassed saying out loud, then likely it will feel more natural as internal dialogue. However, Joannah was able to introduce some private thoughts as external dialogue via a sweet one-way discussion between her main character and her pet turtle.

Think of your rewrite as a fun game where you get to come up with cool, realistic thoughts for your characters or awesome things that they say that will make your reader fall even more in love with your story and the people in it.

Be especially careful not to overdo the internal dialogue. A little can go a long way!

Happy Revising,

Kristi

Kristi Wright is the author of the middle grade, futuristic *Basker Twins in the 31st Century* series. She writes both middle grade and young adult, and in addition to futuristic novels, she loves to write stories with elements of fantasy or magic. She conducts writers' workshops at elementary and middle schools with a focus on students writing with all five senses and a strong character point of view. A Young Inklings teacher and mentor, she lives and writes in Santa Clara, California.

Joannah Cisneros

Joannah is thirteen years old and heading into her high school freshman year. A fine arts enthusiast, she plays the flute and piano, and she dances ballet, tap and jazz. She is looking forward to being a member of her high school's dance squad—the Cavalettes—as well as playing the flute in marching and concert band. Joannah is a big fan of the *Hunger Games* trilogy by Suzanne Collins. Another favorite book is *Love, Aubrey* by Suzanne LaFleur. Joannah lives with her parents, her younger sister and her sweet Cockapoo, Musette, in Oglesby, Illinois.

Here are some of Joannah's thoughts on the writing and revision of "Slaying the Dragon."

What gave you the idea for "Slaying the Dragon"?

At school, I would watch the little kids play and goof around. My younger sister liked to play pretend, too. I got the idea from watching the kids play, and then I put my creative twist on it.

During your revision process, you focused on internal and external dialogue. How did you decide where you wanted to make changes?

I looked at all of the ideas and liked a lot of them. I picked the ones that would explain the story more so that people would better understand the character and what was going on.

How did you feel about revising your story?

I really enjoyed it. I got advice from a professional author! I liked getting ideas for how to make my story better and more understandable. I think it will help me with future writing whether at school or just for fun.

What do you like most about writing?

My mom always says that the fine arts for me are a creative outlet. I have all these ideas in my head, and I'll start thinking of things and writing my ideas down in my notebook. What I like about writing is that you get to be creative and come up with your own little world and story. It's just really fun.

Do you have any advice for other young writers who may be at the beginning of a writing project?

My advice would be to look around at everything you see every day, because everything can inspire you to add more interesting details.

122

Slaying the Dragon

by Joannah Cisneros

124

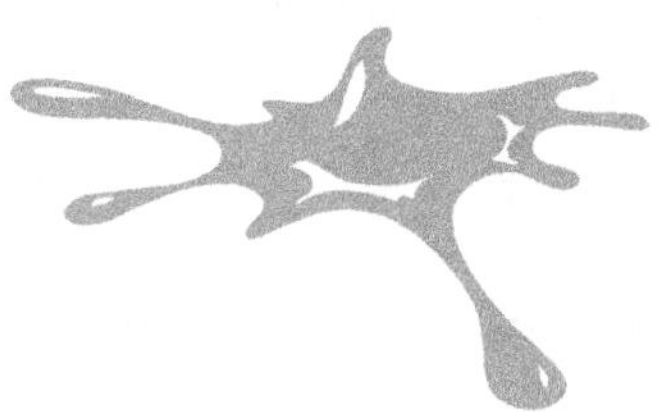

 stare at the clock, waiting patiently for its hands to reach noon. For when the hands reach noon, it is time to go to recess. And I can't wait to see what today's battle brings me.

Mrs. Migilicutti has been explaining something useless that will never help me in life, so I just zoned her out a long while ago.

-RING!-

The loud sound of the bell even startles me. The rest of my class and I jump up off our seats, and rush to get out of the door. But one thing stops me.

"Alexis! I need to speak to you for a minute or two."

I jolt in my path, turn around, and then walk to my teacher's desk.

When all of the students have filed out of the room, I politely say, "Yes, Mrs. Migilicutti."

"I have noticed that you have not been paying attention in my class lately," she says in such a tone that it starts to scare me.

"Oh believe me, Mrs. Migilicutti! I pay so much attention in this class that I think if I even tried to pay attention any more, my brain would pop!"

"Young lady, you are in fourth grade! I do not appreciate all of the sarcasm."

I give a slight frown.

"My point is, if you do not start being a better student, I will have to make you stay inside for recess!"

Her words echo in my brain. Stay inside for recess. Will I ever see the light of day again? Oh, the agony of it all is just too overwhelming.

"Do you understand, Alexis?" Her harsh voice snaps me back to reality.

I gulp and then say, "Yes, ma'am."

"You are dismissed," she says.

I turn, bolt out of the room, go to my cubby, and grab my sword out of my backpack.

I think back to the time when I first made my sword. It was in the beginning of this school year in art class. My favorite teacher, Miss Sanders, helped me make it out of paper towel rolls. Miss Sanders is truly the only person who deeply understands my creativity.

After my quick thought, I go running down the hall at such a speed which causes me to crash into the door. I quickly regain my balance, and calmly pull open the door.

I then stumble upon a sight that will definitely spoil my lunch. The playground starts to transform into something;

its winding shapes start to twist and turn. When its new form becomes clear, I can see that a fire-breathing dragon has come to attack!

I hold my sword out in a guarded position and then go charging at the dragon. But one thing blocks my path: Sally Jeinkins. I have no choice but to hit her with my sword so that she tumbles to the ground, and out of my way. Can you blame me? Sometimes you've got to take one for the team.

I am just about to slice the dragon's head off, when a proper, high-pitched voice stops me, "Alexis! Get over here right now!"

Just at that moment, I know that I'm in big trouble.

I am immediately sent home, and suspended of my recess privileges for a month.

"Alexis, you are grounded!" my mom shouts in an angry tone.

"Grounded!?! I for one think that this is simply outrageous!"

"Tell that to Sally Jeinkins, who now has a large scrape on her face," Mom yells in a sarcastic tone.

I let out a large sigh and turn to go walk to my room.

"Oh, and one more thing," Mom says. She sneaks up behind me and snatches my sword right out of my hands. "This is going into the city-wide dumpster!"

"Mom, no!" I shriek.

Mom shouts to my dad, "Louis, keep an eye on Alexis. I'll be back in a little while."

I abruptly turn, and go running to my room. I plop down on my desk chair and begin ranting on and on to Herman, my pet turtle.

"Nobody understands me, except for you, of course. Sometimes I think it would be much easier to be a turtle like you. Doesn't Mom understand that I was only trying to save the school… if not the whole world from being under the control of that awful dragon?"

I look at Herman, and he seems to cock his head and give me a guilty look. I say, enthralled, "Yeah Herman, maybe I did let my imagination get the better of me this time…but can you blame me? It was just so exciting!"

A week has gone by without recess, battles, and worst of all, my sword. However, with the incredible act that I put up, I think mom is beginning to forgive me.

I am sitting in my room talking to Herman, when I hear my mom call from downstairs, "Alexis, honey, please come down here. I need to talk to you."

I thump loudly down the stairs, and plop onto the couch.

"I have noticed how well you have behaved throughout this past week, and because of your good behavior, I would like to give this to you." From behind her back, she pulls out my sword!

"My sword!" I jump up and run over to her then politely take it out of her hand. "I thought you threw it out?!?"

"Oh honey, I would never do that to you. I know how much that sword means to you," she says sweetly.

"Thanks, Mom!" I say then give her a hug. I then skip happily out of the house, and walk to school.

I finally approach my school, and see enormous, dark clouds surrounding the school. I gulp, grasp my sword tightly in my hands, and rush into school.

Once I pass the main entry, I stumble upon the two,

intersecting hallways. One is glowing a fluorescent green, the other a bright blue. I begin to panic, not knowing which hall to take. I look all around, looking for some sort of hint that will signal which path I should take. I see that my sword is projecting some sort of riddle on the wall.

THERE ARE TWO HALLWAYS, GREEN AND BLUE. YOU MAY NOT BE SURE WHICH TO CHOOSE. SO HERE'S A HINT, FROM ME TO YOU: TAKE THE ONE THAT LEADS YOU TO YOUR BATTLES, IN WHICH YOU NEVER LOSE.

I think to myself… the hall that leads you to your battles. Let me think, the hall that is glowing blue leads to all of the classrooms. The green leads to the computer lab, art room, and…the playground. That's it, the playground!

I grip my sword tightly and go running down the green, glowing hallway. I burst through the doors, and stumble upon the horrific sight of the fire-breathing dragon cornering all of the teachers and students in the playground. I hear a few faint shrieks.

I give out a loud gasp, and when everyone hears it, they turn their heads to me, with pleading looks on their faces, and say, "Alexis, help us!" or things like, "Save us!"

I gulp, and whisper quietly, "This is real."

Then I think to myself, I always knew deep, deep, down that all of my other battles were fake, but this…this is real.

Just as I go to attack, my sword turns into some kind of an amazing gadget with lasers, knives, and other miscellaneous yet helpful items.

I gasp. "Wow!" All along I thought this was just a piece of

cardboard, yet this piece of cardboard has many sentimental values to me. Now it is an astonishing contraption that could help the fate of the school, and doom the fate of the dragon.

I take a deep breath, and go charging at this dreadful creature.

The dragon sees me coming, and lets out a loud roar and blows fire into the air. I go to slice him with the laser, but miss, and accidently slice the playground equipment in half, and it goes tumbling down. The dragon and I chase each other around where the playground equipment used to be. He finally corners me, and out of desperation, I just press a random button. I float way up high in the sky. It must have been a levitation button. From below me, the dragon cannot escape my wrath now.

I suddenly feel guilty, and decide to show him mercy, so I say, "Go dragon, and never come back. If you never come back, I will spare you your life."

That cowardly dragon flies away, and everyone cheers, chanting my name!

I've done it. I have finally slayed the dragon!

THE END

Character Emotion

nn Jacobus mentored Benjamin Huang through a revision focused on developing the character's emotion in Benjamin's story, "The Shakespeare Adventure."

Dear Reader,

In Benjamin Huang's "The Shakespeare Adventure," the great Bard himself is the main character, and a cool one at that. He thinks fast and is an excellent swordsman. While we are privy to some of his thoughts, and we learn much from his actions, before revision we didn't get as much exposure to his innermost feelings. One thing that a fiction writer can provide that a screenwriter, for example, cannot, is the chance to be inside the head and heart of the point-of-view character.

Benjamin looked for this kind of writing in a book he

likes, and cited a section where it was evident to him what the main character is feeling: afraid. How could he tell? Because the character is riding in a car thinking about how his mother is silent and angry at him, and about what he had done in soccer, and about the fear he saw in an old man's eyes and how he understands it; it's how he feels now. Internal dialogue is one important way to show what a character is feeling.

While a writer can certainly state a character's emotions outright, often it's even better to let the reader figure it out for him or herself. One way Benjamin does this well in his story is by what Shakespeare does or says. When he comes back to his table to discover his work gone, then runs after a man yelling, "Stop, thief!" and, "*En garde,*" we can be pretty sure how he is feeling.

Another way to convey emotion is by reporting what the character is doing with his face, hands or body. If someone covers their eyes and holds their head with their hands, what emotion do you suspect they're experiencing? How about tapping a foot and glancing at the wall clock?

Pretend you are frightened and look at yourself in

the mirror. Or think about a time a when a friend was scared. How does someone's mouth look when they're watching something really scary? Their eyes? What do they do with their hands? Squeeze them into fists? Pluck at their armrest? How do they sit or stand? Now think about this for anger, surprise, sadness, excitement and impatience. What other emotions can you identify? You may want to make some notes to use in your work.

In your writing, look at times when the events happening in your story would make your main character feel an emotion, strongly or even slightly. Can other readers identify how your character is feeling? If not, you probably won't need to add much. An internal thought, or often just a single gesture or a facial expression, tells us all we need to know.

Truly yours,

Ann

Ann Jacobus's debut YA thriller will be out from St. Martin's Press/Macmillan in fall 2015. She earned an MFA in Writing for Children and Young Adults from Vermont College of Fine Arts, and has published stories, essays and poems in magazines and anthologies. She and her family live in San Francisco where she teaches writing to kids and adults.

Benjamin Huang

Benjamin is a thirteen-year-old Chinese-American. He likes reading books and eating chicken soup. When he was eight years old, he tried to make his own chicken soup with mixed results. He attends Jane Lathrop Stanford Middle School in California, and has a younger brother and sister.

Here are some of Benjamin's thoughts on the writing and revision of "The Shakespeare Adventure."

How long have you been writing?

I have many half-finished stories I've worked on for the last four or five years. I also took a creative writing class.

Who are some of your favorite authors and/or books? What do you like about them?

Two of my favorite authors are J.K. Rowling, and Eoin Colfer. Recently I've read and liked *Origami Yoda* by Tom Angleburger, *Nick of Time* by Ted Bell, *The Chronicles of Narnia* by C.S. Lewis, and *The Spiderwick Chronicles* by Tony DiTerlizzi and Holly Black. The *Harry Potter* series is an all-around favorite and I've read the whole thing twice. It's really the father (mother?) of all fantasy novels. It's got everything—wizards, magic, potions and evil.

How did you come up with this story idea?

I really had no ideas at first, although I thought I might like to write about a warrior or an artist. Then I got the idea about Shakespeare. I don't plan that much about plot but like to throw my character into a situation and see what happens.

In my research, I couldn't find any specific details on the creation of *Hamlet*. That gave me an opportunity and free range to create a story about how Shakespeare got his ideas. Maybe he got his idea just the way I wrote it in the story.

What kind of person do you imagine that Shakespeare was? What kind of person is he in your story?

I picture Shakespeare as quiet and introverted, sensible, and not a braggart. I have read other books about him and the period such as *The Shakespeare Stealer* by Gary Blackwood which was good historical fiction and inspired me. I also did research in the library and on the web about Shakespeare and London during his time. I've read *Hamlet* and *The Tempest*, and I'm doing a monologue from *The Tempest* (Prospero's epilogue) for drama class.

Are you working on a new story?

Yes. It's about a kid fighting an ancient evil. Whatever he draws, animates and pops out of the paper to help him.

The Shakespeare Adventure

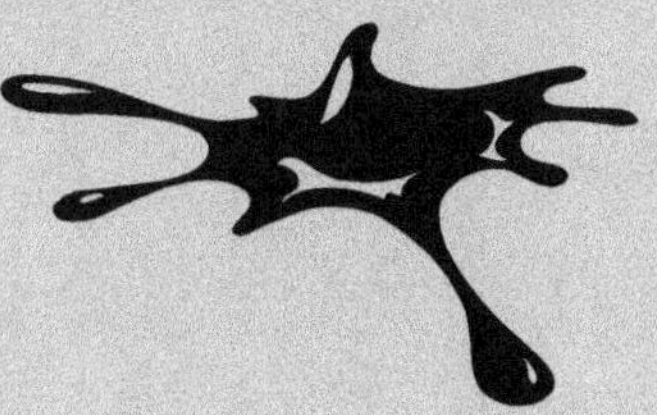

by

Benjamin Huang

138

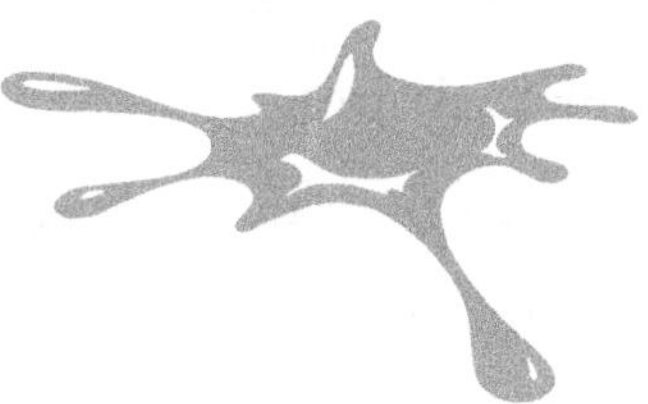

He was stuck. William Shakespeare, brilliant playwright, the man who had been called the most talented writer of his time by his peers, was stymied. He leaned back from his wooden desk, cluttered with quills, bottles of black ink, and crumpled papers spotted with ink like sores on a plague-afflicted man. He looked out the window at the bland grey Renaissance London sky of 1600, and sighed.

The bard was stuck on the plot of the play *Hamlet*, a play that his acting troupe, "The Chamberlain's Men," was set to perform in five days at the Globe theatre, and that deadline was looming closer by the minute. What to do, what to do… He had to give Prince Hamlet, the center of the play, the truth about his uncle Claudius. The bard already knew that Claudius had killed Hamlet's father, the former king, to ascend to kingship. But how should Hamlet discover this truth? Should he stumble upon it mistakenly, or hear it from somebody, but how? And who? Shakespeare sighed and stood up from the desk wearily. He put on his black cloak, thinking that some air would help him.

He stepped out and was immediately hit by the cocktail of London air: smoke from coal fires, the smell of beer from a nearby tavern, dirt, and animal waste from the streets. Shakespeare walked down the street, all the while pondering. He walked past a narrow alley and saw a group of people clustered around something, murmuring in low voices. Against his better judgment, Shakespeare decided to investigate. The crowd surrounding the mystery thing of interest was too thick, so Shakespeare tapped the shoulder of the man nearest.

"What is going on?" he asked.

"Ah, there was a waylaying here. A beggar jumped at a young pair walking back home, the husband thought it was his dead brother. Can't blame him, it was night. But anyways, he tried to embrace the fellow and got it in the ribs. Had the life drained right out of him. The miss screamed something awful and woke half the street. The brigand fled by then," was the bystander's reply.

But the words fell on deaf ears. Shakespeare had had a brainwave. A flood of ideas and thoughts flew into his mind, no doubt triggered by the man's own speech. What if… Hamlet's father himself came? From the dead? And told Hamlet the truth? It made more sense than gossip or a random discovery. Shakespeare thanked the man and hurried out of the alley.

He tore into a tavern and sat down at a table. Immediately, the bard took out a short stubby pencil and a crumpled piece of paper that he kept with him at all times to note down ideas that might come to his head, and began scribbling words down on the parchment furiously, as though the ideas might fly out of his head at any moment. Finally, satisfied that all his ideas were on paper, Shakespeare sat back for a moment. Excited with this story development, he walked over to the bar and ordered a glass of ale. He paid the bartender and strode back to his table, ready for further brainstorming, only to find that the piece of parchment that had been lying there was gone!

A hot rush of fear shot through Shakespeare. He looked under and in the vicinity of the table. Nothing. Then, it must have been taken. But by whom? A common thief? But more likely, a thief in the employment of a rival. After all, there were playwrights like Ben Jonson and Christopher Marlowe, people who had disliked his rise to fame in London. He rushed to the door, and saw a figure in a grey cloak rushing down the street.

Shakespeare ran after him, shouting "Stop, thief! Stop that man!"

The figure, realizing that his escape had not been clean, rushed into an alleyway in the hopes of losing his pursuer in the maze of London's streets and alleys. But Shakespeare did not let up the chase. Suddenly, the figure tripped over one of the uneven cobblestones that made up the road. Shakespeare caught up just as the figure, who was wearing a mask with a nose resembling a beak, scrambled up and unsheathed a long silver rapier hidden in his belt.

"Do not follow me any further, sir, or you will feel the point of this blade," said the masked figure in a muffled voice.

The bard knew that to get back the parchment, he would have to fight this man for it, or give up.

So, Shakespeare drew his own rapier, intoning, "En garde."

The masked figure swung, and the duel was on. Their blades

clinked and clanked, making a ringing sound in the narrow alleyway. By now, several passersby had gathered to watch the duel. Shakespeare knew that he would have to end this soon, or else the constables would arrive and they would both be incarcerated for questioning, so he would have to act fast. Quickly, the bard stepped back and kicked out at a dirty puddle, spraying water into his opponent's eyes and momentarily blinding him. Next, Shakespeare jumped up and flicked his blade up to a washing line that hung between the pair of apartment buildings that made up the alleyway. As a result, a wet dress fell upon his opponent's head. The thief writhed and struggled to remove the heavy, wet cloth from his face, swearing indignantly. Almost grinning at the man's comical appearance, Shakespeare sliced into the man's thigh and knocked him onto the ground, keeping his sword-tip pointed at the man's throat.

"Who is your employer?" he asked sternly, as a rush of triumph and a bit of puzzlement washed over him from the successful duel.

The thief's only reply was a muffled curse. The bard was about to reply with a scathing remark, when he heard the clatter of boots on cobblestones and knew that the constables had no doubt been alerted to the duel and were coming. He quickly searched the thief and in about five seconds, his hand had closed around a crumpled ball of parchment. And Shakespeare was off, running down the alley, the thief's muffled screams hurrying him on his way.

Once he made sure that he was safe, Shakespeare unrolled the crumpled piece of paper that he had snatched out of the man's pocket. One was his notes on *Hamlet*, the other was a description of the bard, where he lived, and a few instructions. It seemed that the man had been tailing the bard for days, evidently trying to gather evidence on Shakespeare's plays or any other information. The unknown employer had not put his name down, only X.

In the evening, with a crackling fire in the hearth and the sounds of London drifting through his window, the bard reflected upon the day's activities. As his eyelids drooped closed and a calming warmth came over him, a final thought lingered in his head for a moment: Who was the man behind this? But that was a mystery for another day.

THE END

144

Building to a Climax

Mandy Davis mentored Suvali Chadha through a revision focused on choosing a central story in Suvali's story, "The Adventures of Anna Hazelberry."

Dear Reader,

The climax of a story is the highest point of action. It's the moment near the end of a story when the main character finally solves her problem. Think about a pyramid. Think about the stone at the very top of that pyramid. That stone could not be there without all the other stones supporting it. In the same way, the climax of your story must be supported by the rest of your story. This is why you must *build up to your climax.*

One way to build up to a climax is to have a strong central problem in your story. In Suvali Chadha's

"The Adventures of Anna Hazelberry," readers learn immediately that Anna has been kidnapped and know that Anna's main goal in the story is to escape her captors. We see Anna try to escape multiple times during the story. Each time Anna tries to escape and fails, we are *building to the climax*. Each failure to solve her problem raises the tension and makes me want to keep reading to see how Anna finally escapes her kidnappers. So, look back at your story and see how many times your main character tries to solve her problem before she actually solves it. If your main character tries and fails only once or not at all, consider adding a failure or two. Each failure will help build up to a more exciting climax.

Another important aspect of the climax is giving the main character an *active* role in solving the problem. The main character should solve her problem using one of her strengths or something she learns during the course of the story. So, check your climax. Does the main character luck into a solution to the problem? In Suvali's original version of "The Adventures of Anna Hazelberry," Anna escapes by happening upon a loose bar in her cell. Suvali revised her story so that Anna escapes by convincing the nephew of her captors to let

her go free. In the new version, Anna relies on one of her strengths, her intelligence, to help her escape. This new climax is much more satisfying for the reader!

Remember, revising the climax of your story isn't just about rewriting. It's about rereading the story, thinking about what you've already written, and then making the changes.

Happy revising!

Mandy

Mandy Davis is the author of the forthcoming middle grade novel *Stuperstar*. She has an MFA in Writing for Children and Young Adults from Hamline University and has taught writing at the elementary and middle school levels for six years. She lives and writes in Minneapolis, Minnesota.

Suvali Chadha

Suvali is a fourth grader at North Hillsborough Elementary School. She has a red fox Labrador named Zeus. She likes to play piano and soccer. Suvali enjoys cooking, especially her famous tiramisu. She also enjoys traveling. Her favorite destination is the Maldives where she can often be found swimming and snorkeling.

Here are some of Suvali's thoughts on the writing and revision of "The Adventures of Anna Hazelberry."

What changes did you make to your climax?

In my old climax, Anna escapes on her own after finding a loose bar in her cell. In the new climax, instead of escaping on her own, I made Anna convince Jack to let her out. Now she is relying in someone else to help her get out of the cell.

How did thinking about Anna's strengths help you create a new climax?

In my new climax, Anna has to convince Jack to let her out of the cell. You have to be smart to convince someone to do something, and being smart is one of Anna's strengths.

She is relying on her own wits to figure out the solution to her problem.

Why do you like your new ending better?

In the first ending, Anna just stumbles onto the solution to her problem by finding the loose bar in the cell and getting out that way. In the new ending, Anna doesn't just stumble upon a solution to her problem. She has to think of a solution that gets her out. I think my new ending is better because it's more interesting. If I were reading a book where a character just happened to find her way out, it would feel like more of a classic ending. My ending feels more original.

How do you come up with your story ideas?

I get a lot of my story ideas from books. I also get ideas from other people. I started this story last year in a Young Inklings class. I got the idea for Anna being kidnapped from my Inklings teacher. She was also writing a story about someone getting kidnapped. When I was trying to figure out what to name my character, one of my friends helped me think of the last name Hazelberry. We both loved that name!

What advice would you give other students about revision?

Your writing will not always be perfect. It is always possible to improve. Young writers can get a lot of inspiration from other people. You should always be grateful for the constructive criticism because it really does help!

150

The Adventures of Anna Hazelberry

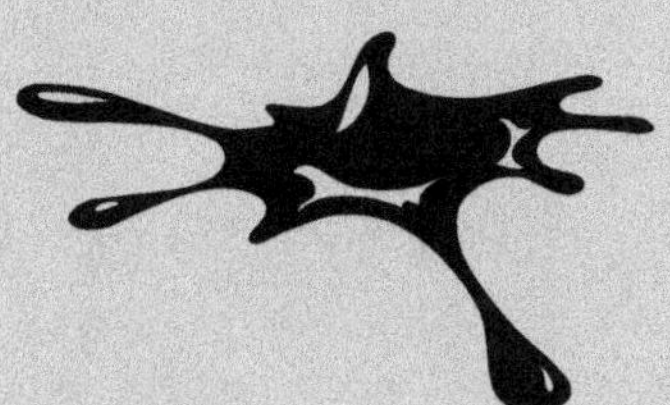

by Suvali Chadha

152

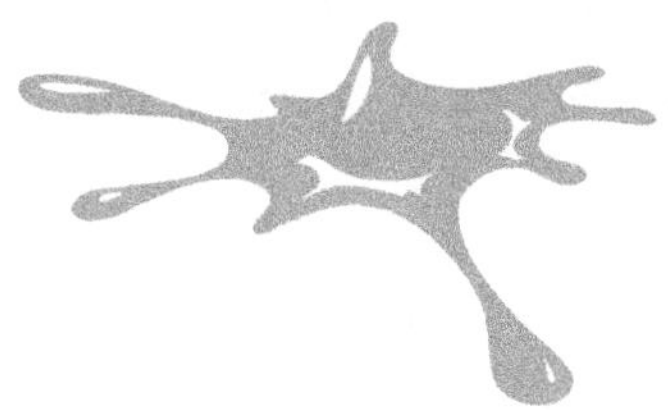

Let me gooooooo!"

Five minutes ago, I was simply stargazing while eating a pack of marshmallows and sitting on my front yard porch. Now I'm being dragged across my porch into a big black van by three people in black masks. Did I mention the part about a black van and black masks? I scream again. Ugh, why do our next-door neighbors have to be such deep sleepers? Dumb neighbors!

Once they drag me into the big black (did I mention the part about it being a very creepy) van, I successfully punch one thug in the face. But in my moment of victory, Thug #2 manages to tie my hands, while Thug #3 recovers, and Thug #1 starts the engine. It's sort of cute how I named them Thug #1, Thug #2 and Thug #3, huh? Not.

Thug #2 (he seems to be the boldest) says, "Gag the brat!"

I reply, "Am not! You shouldn't even be talking because you're a stu-mphhhph—"

Great, I've been gagged.

"Feet next?" Thug #3 (the one I punched) asks. I lash out with my foot and kick his stomach, and then he doubles over as the van makes a turn.

"We're here!" Thug #1 calls out.

And only then do I realize he has an accent, and I'm pretty sure it's Spanish. Then somebody waves a sickeningly sweet-smelling napkin in front of me. And (of course) I faint.

When I wake up, I find myself in what seems to be a prison cell. I immediately notice that all three thugs aren't present. And the only signs of life in the dreary, dusty, despicable kidnapper's den are the gray-furred red-eyed rats running across the den and a boy about my age peeling potatoes in a corner.

"Hey," I say.

The boy is so startled he nearly drops his potato peeler. He looks up at me.

"So you're our new guest?" he says.

I don't like the way he says the word *guest*.

"More like prisoner. I was just home alone and then your friends had to come along and kidnap me!" I practically shout.

"Oh, yeah, about that, ummm… well, I'm Jack. You're?"

I glare at him. "My name is Anna, Anna Hazelberry and I'm not pleased to meet you. And just for the record you stink at changing the subject."

He squints at me. "You're… you're…"

"Awesome? Wonderful? Better than you?" I reply.

"I was going towards annoying."

I stare daggers at him.

"Listen up, potato boy, you and your pals made a big mistake. When my parents find me here you're gonna be in big trouble!!!"

He jumps up from the vegetable crate he was sitting on, and just as he's about to open his mouth and yell something, the door opens and a middle-aged man with brown hair strides in. As soon as Jack sees the man come in, he plops back on the vegetable crate as if nothing ever happened.

"Hello," he says, and I recognize his voice as Thug # 1's, the driver.

"Where are your friends?" I ask.

"Joining us soon," he replies.

He's right. Only a few seconds later, the door opens again and two more men walk into the room. The first one has a short, stocky figure and the second one is tall and skinny with a bruise on his face. The one with the bruise on his face groans.

"I don't want to do the imitation. My bruise hurts," he complains. "Well, that's too bad. I told you to ice it!" the short one yells.

The brown-haired man takes a step forward.

"Calm down, Winston. It's not Harry's fault, it's the little kid's fault." he says.

"You're right, Miguel. It's the brat's fault!" Winston snarls.

I gasp. Winston was Thug #2, the one who called me a brat yesterday night! And Harry must be Thug #3, but there are a few things I don't get:

1) Why does Harry a.k.a Thug #3 have a bruise on his face?

2) What imitation are they talking about and whom are they

imitating?

3) Why am I here?

Harry must have seen me staring at his bruise, because he glares at me and says, "Remember, little girl, YOU did this to me."

That proves it. He has to be Thug #3, because I punched Thug #3 in the face last night! I allow a wave of triumph to wash over me as I flex my hands in awe. Not bad for an eleven-yea-old, huh?

Miguel begins, "I want you to keep an eye on the girl, understand? And don't touch the models or maps, they're the plans for you-know-what," he adds.

Jack doesn't respond but simply nods his head. Miguel then gives me a chilling final glare and leaves the room with a quick glance at the "plans."

As soon as he leaves, I try to get a closer look at the plans. Annoyingly, Jack doesn't let me.

"I would appreciate it if you would just move," I say.

"In your dreams." He smirks.

In my frustration, I throw a rock from the circle of them in my cell at Jack's foot and he stumbles backwards, crashing into the plans. After a few seconds, he scrambles up and looks at the damage that he has inflicted. The sight is not a pretty one. The maps are scattered on the floor, thumbtacks are bent and broken into tiny shards, and the table holding everything has fallen and crushed every remaining object. Jack whirls around.

"Please don't tell I broke it! Please?" he pleads.

I sense my opportunity right away.

"On two conditions. One: You have to tell me the plan and

why I'm here. Two: You have to get me out of here!"

He agrees without hesitation, but then he pauses and replies, "But they can't know I helped you."

"Duh," I say.

"Okay. Well, I'll start with my story 'cause it sorta ties in with the story you're asking for," he starts.

"Sure," I agree.

"Good. Well, it all started when my teacher got sick, and my class had a substitute. She was a mean old hag, so one of my classmates popped a Mentos into her Coke bottle. Then I shook it up. And when she opened it, it burst, and then we got into big, big trouble. So while my parents are in Rio I have to stay with my uncle 'cause they know I want to go to Rio." He pauses to take a breath and then continues.

"My uncle is really mean. He told me the plan, but that was only if I didn't tell anyone. Obviously I broke that promise."

"Just get to the part about why I'm here," I interrupt.

"Fine, you're here because my uncle's crew wants to get a ransom out of your parents," he says.

"But how would they know I was actually here? I wouldn't say it in my own voice," I ask.

"Be patient. So, as I was saying, the guy with the bruise on his face is going to imitate you. And since your parents are rich and all, they're gonna get a big heap of money."

I sit in the cell for a while and think about the information I was just told. Then I come to a no-brainer conclusion.

"Now you have to get me out of here!"

He smiles.

"Okay!" he says. Then he picks up an insanely sharp rock and throws it at my foot. I move my foot away just in time.

"What was that for?" I yell.

"What do you mean, what was that for? I got you out," he says, grinning mischievously.

"Obviously you didn't get me out, because I'm still in this cell!" I respond angrily.

"Oh, well, you said, 'get me out of here,' when you were sitting inside that circle of rocks, remember?"

I groan. I've been tricked.

"But can you still get me out of this cell just as an act of kindness?" I beg. "And anyways, I can still tell your uncle about how you knocked over the plans!"

"No, and who do you think they'll believe more? Me or you?" he asks with a satisfied grin.

And just as he is about to leave, I yell, "Jack!"

He turns around.

"What is it now?" he mutters, obviously annoyed.

"You want to go to Rio, right? Well, I could get you a plane ticket to Rio," I say.

"What do I have to do for you?" he asks, raising an eyebrow. I swallow.

"If you let me go, I'll do all of that and I'll also get the police to arrest your uncle and crew. Please?"

His reply startles me.

"I don't need to go to Rio. Just get rid of my uncle and his friends so I can go back to my old life."

Then he steps forward and unlocks my cell.

"Go," he says.

And I run out the door away from prison cells, and toward freedom.

Happiness flows through me like a wave and I look around. Weirdly, I'm surrounded by a parking lot and a small grass field. I smile. I'm almost free. I just have to get home! I step out of the building and look around. According to the street sign, I'm on Wire Lane! Just my luck. I only live two blocks away from Wire Lane! I run as fast as possible down the street and home. A feeling of relief washes over me, and I reach for the door handle. Finally, my mom opens the door, and after multiple hugs and kisses, she brings me inside, and I explain what had happened to me.

"Anna," she begins "I think you should take a nap."

"But mom we ha-"

"Anna, go take a nap and everything will be all right," she interrupts.

I sigh and climb the stairs to my bedroom. Then, as if chanting a prayer, my mom whispers, "Everything will be all right."

THE END

160

Character Details

Frances Lee Hall mentored Kaya Shin-Sherman through a revision focused on character details in Kaya's story, "Voyage to America."

Dear Reader,

Kaya's story, "Voyage to America," tells the tale of Abram, a young boy emigrating from Russia to the United States in the early 1900s. Through journal entries, Abram writes about leaving his homeland for the first time, and encountering difficult experiences. I found myself caring about Abram very much. I felt his anxiety about traveling into the unknown. At the same time, I wanted to know more about him.

We decided our revision focus would be on developing strong character details, so that by the story's end, readers can have a fuller appreciation for Abram's inner and outer journey. I also asked Kaya to write a new, final paragraph to help bring this intriguing story to a satisfying conclusion. And developing character details would help her do this.

You may have heard the expression, "it's all in the details." And it's true! Every detail has a purpose, no matter how big or small. Details help readers understand, empathize with, or even judge our characters. It is often in the small details that reveal character, and can impact how the story moves forward.

Start with the basics. Know details like age, gender, or where a character lives to ground readers in your character's here and now. A teen waitress living in her mom's station wagon conjures up different emotions than a third grade prince living in a palace. In Kaya's revisions, she added that Abram would miss his shtetl, which gives a sense that he is traveling all the way from Eastern Europe to America.

A writing teacher once told me you can learn a lot about a character by what she carries in her pocket. Choose

and write down specific objects or details that only your character would carry. Or what your character is forced to carry. Think Harry Potter and his wand. Or Katniss and her bow and arrow. The more specific, the better. Kaya revised by adding that Abram chooses to take along his quilted handkerchief made out of his family clothes, sewn by his grandmother. These rich details represent Abram's life at home, and suggest he will miss someone special, his grandmother.

Character details add depth, create reader empathy, and move your story forward to a satisfying conclusion. Have fun picking and choosing the exact details that are specific, meaningful, and deserving of your unique character.

Keep on Writing,

Frances

Frances Lee Hall's debut middle grade novel, *Fried Wonton* (working title), is forthcoming from Egmont USA in 2015. She earned an MFA in Writing for Children and Young Adults from Vermont College of Fine Arts. Additional work includes a TV broadcast and video producer and writer, and book reviewer.

Kaya Shin-Sherman

Kaya is a third grader in Palo Alto. In her free time, she loves reading, biking, and playing outdoors. She likes to sew fake food out of cloth, such as pea-pods with three faces, a watermelon that fits in a case, and a PB&J sandwich. One series she really enjoys is the Little House series, by Laura Ingalls Wilder.

Here are some of Kaya's thoughts on the writing and revision of "Voyage to America."

What were the main changes you made in your story?

I talked more about Gabriele and his language, and more about him.

What about the quilted handkerchief?

When I added the handkerchief, I was thinking about how this would make Abram feel. And why he brought it. And I thought that maybe this is meaningful to him. And it will remind him of his family. So that basically shows he cares about his family and he wants to remember them when he is away from them.

What was your process in developing the final, new paragraph?

I was thinking about things that make me happy. And I like playing in snow, but I barely get to go in snow, so that makes me extra happy. So I thought that might be good for this paragraph. So they were playing in snow and having fun and all is great. The snow, I guess, is sort of a symbol of happiness and fun. And everything's going to be okay. And I mention how happy he is.

Which character detail helped you to see your character differently?

When I added that Gabriele's language is smooth and rolling, and how Abram's Russian is smooth, but abrupt, that made me feel like that Gabriele is more gentle and smooth, and calm and stuff. But Abram can be a little more like, energetic, like bursts of energy.

What was the most challenging part of revising this story?

I think when I added that whole new section at the end. I had to brainstorm a long time, thinking of where and when and what they would be doing when he thought about all the stuff that he's happy about. 'Cause it was a whole new section.

Why did you decide to write this story?

I wrote this story because I wanted readers to know how immigration was in the 1900s. Because I don't think a lot of people know about it. They know about bigger things that happened. I guess immigration is a big thing, but not everybody learns about it. I think readers will be interested in this.

We learned a lot about immigration at school. And so we went to Angel Island, which is where most Asian people went to. We wrote research papers about immigration; and I wrote about immigrants who became famous people. Like Joseph Pulitzer, who became a very important person in a newspaper.

How did you feel about needing to make revisions?

At first I was a little bit disappointed because I thought my piece was pretty good. When I looked back, and looked at the questions, and looked at my paper, I realized that it wasn't so perfect. And I just got used to it, and I became fine with it.

If a fellow writer friend of yours didn't want to do revisions, what advice would you give that person?

I would tell them, maybe people won't like your book because it isn't as good as it might be if you revise it. And even though you feel like you don't want to do it, or you can't do it… I encourage you. You should do it.

What do you like most about writing?

I like how you can make up a lot of stuff. Or you can shape a story around something you know. Like this story. 'Cause I know a lot about immigration, so I shaped the story. My background knowledge about immigration is the mold, and the filling for the mold is the story.

Do you have another story you'd like to work on?

I'd like to write a story about someone on the *Titanic*, because I'm really interested in historical fiction. Even though the experience was pretty freaky, it would be super awesome to be there then, and to experience that. No one I know, or no one anyone knows now went on the *Titanic*. It's really interesting to hear about it. And know how it feels.

Voyage to America

by Kaya Shin-Sherman

168

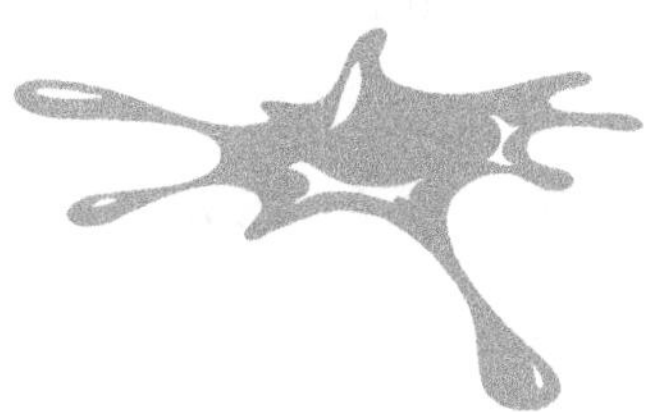

*pril 30, 1917*

Mother says we will only be able to pack one belonging to bring to America. It is hard to decide what to bring. To make it easier, I am deciding what not to bring first. My school work will not come to America. My school bag and uniform will not be coming either. Textbooks, play sets, writing materials, and most of my books won't come. Of course, my chair, small desk, and lamp are going to be sold with lots of other furniture. I do not like having everything I've ever known being sold. I don't want to leave the *shtetl*, where the only people I know come from—all my friends.

I don't know anything about this place called "The Golden Land" or America, which concerns me. I have decided to bring a quilted handkerchief made out of my family's clothes. Grandmother sewed it for me. We did not have enough money to bring Grandmother along. It saddens my heart to think about it.

Sincerely,

Abram

*J*uly 17, 1917

Time has been slowly dragging on in this sickening ship overflowing with disease. No one can recall how many days we have been here. I worry for Tanya. She has always been the weakest of us. I am afraid that she will get sick. I can feel regret creeping up my spine and filling my heart with sorrow until it sinks. The food here is putrid. The soup is watery and thin. The vegetables are old and brown. They smell. But even though the food is disgusting, I hope our journey will end soon.

Sometimes, on rare, sunny days, we emigrants are allowed to enjoy some time in the fresh air of the third class deck. There, we like to play games, talk, read, dance, sing, enjoy the view, and a lot more. People hang their clothing out along the railing to dry. I have found a new friend, Gabriele, to play with when the skies grow dark and rain comes.

Gabriele is from Italy. We do not know each other's language, so we talk to each other using hand signs and drawings. I draw a picture of my family to show Gabriele. His Italian language is smooth and rolling. My Russian is smooth but abrupt. He showed me an Italian card game called "Scopa." He promised me that he would teach me how to play some day.

Gabriele's uncle is ill. He has been ill for eight days. The poor man lies in bed, sometimes wriggling as if there are ants in his clothes. He grips the frayed edge of his quilts until his knuckles turn white. You can hear the horrid sound of him forcing harsh breaths out of his mouth. When he lies still, I am afraid that if I put my hand to his chest, I will not feel the solid pound of his heart. I must go to bed now. It is almost 9:30 on Papa's pocket watch.

Sincerely,

Abram

*S*eptember 26, 1917

There is a light drizzle outside. The wind howls sorrowfully. The thin metal roof of our tiny tenement leaks onto the dark wood floor. I look out the window at the cramped tenement buildings. A whiff of fresh air leaks into my nose. I stroke my sister Tanya's damp hair. In the morning, her face was bright pink with fever, so I stayed home from work and Papa, Mama, and Mikhail went to their jobs.

Uncle got injured at the ribbon factory a few days ago. Mikhail visits every day after school, for I have night school with Papa and Mama, and I don't have the time to visit. I wish Gabriele could come over from next door. I hope next time I write in this journal, it will be with better news.

Sincerely,

Abram

December 29, 1917

Today it snowed. This was the first time (in December) that Mama let us play in it. Me, Mikhail, and Gabriele threw balls of snow at each other. Later, we went inside and drank hot tea. I am finally contented with my life: I have a great friend, a small but cozy home, loving parents, and two caring siblings. I am lucky to have what I have, which is a lot compared to when we were in back-home Russia.

Sincerely,

Abram

Building a Conflict

Polly McCann mentored Natalie Wong through a revision focused on character details in Natalie's story, "A Silly Putty's Life."

Dear Reader,

Natalie's creative and funny story, "A Silly Putty's Life," was a joy to read. We chose Building a Conflict as our revision theme. The conflict is the problem that begins your story, and it must be changed or resolved by the end.

Natalie built a fictional world that is fun and funny— one where the reader wants to come and stay awhile. In that wonderful world is a set of characters that have good dialogue that move the story forward. I asked Natalie to work on the foundational details of her characters—their likes and dislikes. This would help build the conflict in the mind of the reader from the beginning of the story.

The conflict: Natalie's characters were presented with a situation they hated, one that could possibly turn deadly. Since they were not human, it was hard to know how much danger the Silly Putties were in. I asked Natalie to make sure her readers first knew what her characters liked, disliked, and what would truly hurt them.

You can do the same type of revision Natalie did: First, think about your main characters from the viewpoint of someone who doesn't know them at all. Next, ask yourself the questions below using your imagination to fill in more details.

- What makes your main characters happy, or what do they enjoy? What would hurt them the most?
- Who (What) changes or solves the conflict?

Natalie's characters had so much personality that I asked her to give them names, especially since they had dialogue. Her main character was a hero who solved

the conflict with the help of a friend. Names gave the characters even more pizzazz. It clarified the conflict and action in the story. This made the characters easier to picture and their actions also easier to visualize. Natalie found that when she named the characters and identified their likes and dislikes very clearly, she built up the conflict so that it appeared more serious to the reader from the beginning. Then when she came to the climax and the resolution she had already written so well, she found her imagination free to explore the special talents of the Silly Putties more deeply. I guess it was like her imagination went into high definition. Wow, I was amazed. Try it for yourself, and see what happens in the world of your story.

Keep writing,

Polly

Polly McCann, artist and writer, received her MFA in writing from Hamline University. She studied poetry under Julia Kasdorf and workshopped with Ron Koertge. Currently she is working on several biographies, novels, and books of poetry. *Tea with Alice* is the title for her collection of autobiographical poems; three generations of stories retold in free verse. You can find her under a rainbow in Kansas City with her two children and their dog, Spencer.

Natalie Wong

Natalie is in second grade at Keys School She enjoys playing soccer and piano. She can speak Chinese, and a little bit of Korean and Spanish. Her favorite color is blue. Her favorite animal is a horse because horses are fast! Natalie lives in Los Altos, California, where she keeps a growing collection of her very own Silly Putty.

Here are some of Natalie's thoughts on the writing and revision of "A Silly Putty's Life."

What was it like to add more details about the Silly Putties' likes and dislikes?

It was sort of fun and sort of hard because I had to look at everything and think of what I wanted to change and put in.

Did this make the conflict of the story more clear to the reader?

Yes.

When you added names to your Silly Putty characters, did you feel differently about them? For example, how did it change the way you pictured them in your head?

For the narrator—before, he seemed funny. But because of

his name (Tidal Wave). I felt like he was a little more serious. I liked how he changed. And yes, it changed how they looked in my head. Before, it was like a blob of stuff, but now it's a blob of stuff that is blue.

The conflict in your story reaches a climax when the Silly Putties have to hide. You revised your story with new details so that they changed shape and flew into hiding. How did you come up with this new revision, and what did you think about this process?

I liked it. How I came up with it, is that falcons are the fastest birds in the world and the Silly Putties need to get there fast. So I changed it—that made me feel good.

178

A Silly Putty's Life

by Natalie Wong

180

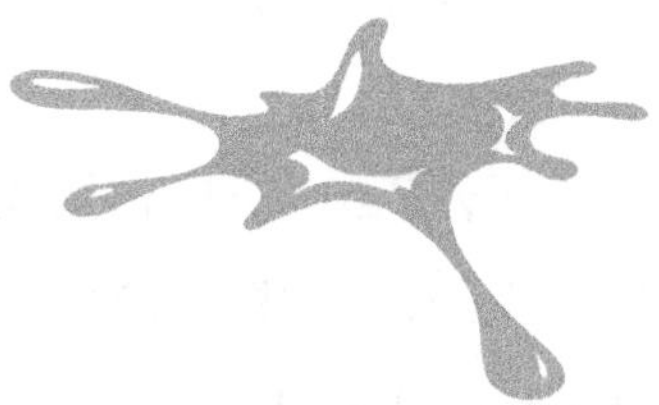

Hello! Nice day, isn't it? My name is Tidal Wave. I am your typical Silly Putty, but I have the most extraordinary human friends. Their names are Jimmy and Lyn. I like them because they stretch and smash me. My life is quite interesting. I think you would like it very much.

Did you know that human beings think water is good? Well, they are very wrong, wrong, wrong. Water is, in fact, the very ticket to death for us Silly Putties. Well, maybe not exactly death but it's pretty bad. We get paralyzed for the rest of our lives!

Once I saved our world from extinction with my Silly Putty friends' help. Let me tell you all about it.

It all began with a bad idea. I mean, a really bad and very unusual idea. The human beings wanted to mix parts of different Silly Putties together and see what color would come out. If the Silly Putties were the same color, life would be okay, but if they were different colors, they would be unhappy. And if one Silly Putty is unhappy for a week, they die. This mixing was another one-way ticket to death! Luckily, I knew the secret for signaling danger.

When I told my Silly Putty friend, Chameleon Green, about the human beings' bad idea, he said, "Tidal Wave, we must save the Silly Putties of our kind and protect their lives!" We wanted to help save our kind so we devised a set of plans:

PLAN A

* Prepare tools.

* Write a sign that says: "DON'T TRY THE IDEA WITH SILLY PUTTY!!!"

PLAN B

* If PLAN A does not work, get all the Silly Putty into hiding.
* Make sure the owners forget about the idea BEFORE revealing the Silly Putty.

Then, we put Plan A into action. We prepared the tools, wrote the sign and laid it out for the humans to see. When Jimmy and Lyn came home from school, they looked around as they always did. They suddenly spotted the sign and their eyes were glued to it.

"Who do you think wrote it?" whispered Jimmy.

"I don't know," answered Lyn.

They walked over to the sign and picked it up. Chameleon Green and I held our breath and waited. Jimmy and Lyn discussed it in whispers.

"What does it mean?" asked Jimmy.

"I don't know," replied Lyn.

"Do you think we should listen?" asked Jimmy.

"I don't know who wrote it but I don't like the sound of it," said Lyn.

"Maybe it's a life and death problem, and that would be bad -- really bad. I think it sounds serious," said Jimmy.

"Well, I don't think so," Lyn responded.

"Actually, you're probably right. I'm going to dunk my Silly Putty in water for the science fair anyway."

Uh-oh. Time to put Plan B into action!

My friend and I hopped out of sight and spread the word to our fellow Silly Putties. We told them our secret code for danger:

DHQ (D = Danger, H = Hide, Q = Quickly!)

Our neighbors opened their doors with worried looks on their faces. Soon, we had a parade of putty following us into the hideout. We got there by fast flying as peregrine falcons, the fastest fliers in the animal kingdom. We Silly Putties can change into whatever we feel like. For example, if someone were feeling sleepy, she might change into a Silly Putty sloth!

We led them to a hole in a tree with a secret entrance that was found years and years ago by a Silly Putty named Quicksilver. The hole was a special hideout, known only to the Silly Putties and somewhere no human being had ever dared to look. After everybody was inside, we quickly but quietly shut the door.

THREE WEEKS LATER....

"Tidal Wave, when are we going to get out of this place?" complained Wendell, one of the Silly Putties.

"Soon," I answered.

"When is soon?" he asked again.

I groaned. Keeping Wendell quiet was like trying to teach a tiger to keep its mouth shut.

"Fine, I'll check," I responded.

"Yes!" he shouted.

I carefully peeked outside. Jimmy and Lyn were going about their usual ways. The reason I knew they forgot about the idea is because they weren't saying: "Where's the putty?" Meanwhile, some fellow Silly Putties took turns peeking outside to observe the humans.

That evening, I gathered all of their reports and not a single one of them said that they heard the humans ask: "Where's the putty?" They must have forgotten about their idea!

I was so excited to share the good news that I decided to make a speech. Wendell and I called every member of the Silly Putty community together. I was tingling with nervousness and excitement.

"Citizens of Puttyland! I am proud to say that we can go out into the world again!" I exclaimed.

A procession of cheers went up from the crowd below. Once again, we led a parade of putty, but this time back to their homes.

Two days later, Jimmy and Lyn had another idea that included Silly Putty. Not again! Time to put our set of plans into action! You won't believe what they wanted to try this time.

THE END

Hold on! Before I tell you that story, I have to tell you something important. I don't mean to brag, but the Silly Putties were so thankful for my leadership that they made me their Chief Silly Putty.

THE END

(This time, for real.)

186

& the Setting Five Senses

Elizabeth Jellison mentored Amann Mahajan through a revision focused on showing emotion through action in Amann's story, "A Walk With Friends & Monkeys."

Dear Reader,

Because the setting of Amann Mahajan's story is so important to the plot, we chose to focus our revision process on setting and the five senses.

The setting is more than just the backdrop to a story. It is the world where the characters live. Just like our world is important, with lots of things to see, smell, taste, touch, and hear, so is the world of the story.

When writing for the senses, playing around with descriptive words is a good way to start. Some words have more feeling to them than others, so a good strategy would be to read your story out loud and think about where you might be able to add a word that better describes how you want your reader to imagine where the story takes place. A thesaurus or a list of descriptive words can really help you with this.

Another thing to think about is which senses you have used a lot in your description, and which senses might need to show up more in your work. What the characters see and touch are often the easiest sensory details to add. But consider adding more of what the setting allows your character to hear, taste, and, smell, too.

One way to see more clearly which senses you're using in your description is to choose a color for each of the five senses. Underline details with color. For instance, if it is something you might see, underline in red. If it's something you'd hear, underline in blue. After a little underlining, your page will look like a rainbow.

(Hopefully!) You'll be able to see what senses you might not be using as much as others. Then, you can brainstorm other details to add to your setting description to fill in the gaps.

Remember, it is better to have a few really juicy words than too many. Your readers can get overwhelmed!

Happy Writing!

Elizabeth

Elizabeth Jellison has a B.A in Arts and Letters for Portland State University in Oregon. After working in a myriad of fields, she has found her calling in teaching writing to children. She lives with her husband and two cats in the Bay Area.

Amann Mahajan

Amann is eight years old and a third grader at El Carmelo Elementary School in Palo Alto. She has no pets but if she could, she would like to have a squirrel. She likes writing and her favorite color is turquoise. She also has a younger brother named Kabir.

Here are some of Amann's thoughts on the writing and revision of "A Walk with Friends & Monkeys."

What shifted or changed when you revised, adding more senses into your story?

> There is more happening—feeling, touching, and smelling. I've seen monkeys eating bananas in Shimla before!

How did you add more senses into the setting of your story?

> I came up with adjectives and descriptive words that worked in the setting.

Why do you enjoy writing?

Because it's fun and you get to put in all your imagination and whatever you want. You can put in whatever you feel, and whatever you're thinking about.

How do you come up with ideas for your stories?

Something happens to me or an idea pops into my head and I make it into a story

Are you working on a new story?

I just finished a story about a teddy bear who's looking for a home and finds lots of friends. It's about friendship.

Where do you like to write?

I like to write at the dining table or at a counter on blank paper. I like to write with a pencil.

A Walk with Friends & Monkeys

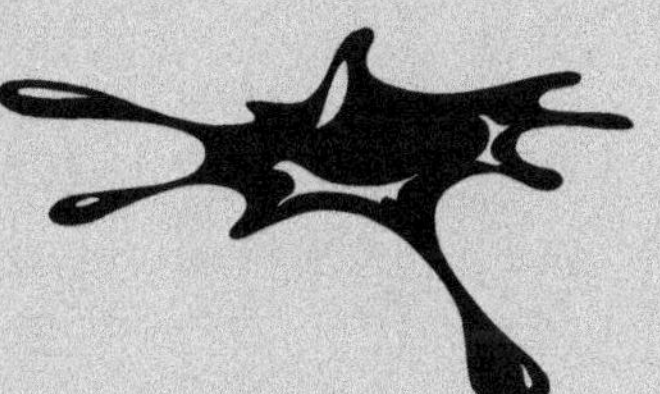

by

Amann Mahajan

194

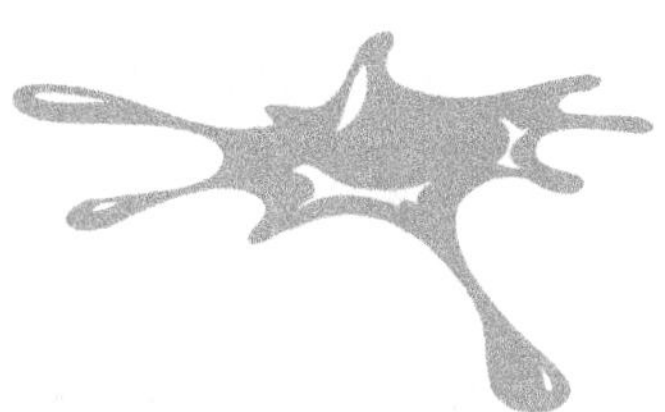

omal lived in Shimla, India. She was a pretty girl with bright, laughing eyes and long dark braids to her waist. Shimla was in northern India, a place with tall, elegant mountains and lots of chilly weather. There were many green chinar trees and pine trees there.

It was a partly warm, and a partly chilly day. Komal had worked hard at school that day and now she wanted to take the pleasure of a treat. A walk to the Mahajan store for snacks would be the perfect thing! The Mahajan store was near the side of the trail that Komal and her friends were going to walk up. The store looked shabby with its broken windows and old brown wood, but people went to that store to buy luscious sweets and other everyday things. Bushy pine trees surrounded the store.

Komal pulled on her jacket, ready to go on a walk with her

friends, Nakul and Tara, and her brother Sohum.

"Hurry up!" she said excitedly. "The shop closes at four forty-five."

She licked her lips as she imagined those chewy toffee rolls. "Yum," Komal said aloud.

"What?" asked Nakul, turning to Komal.

"Nothing," Komal said, still dreaming of toffee rolls.

You might not have guessed this, but Komal could not resist food. Even if she was really full, she couldn't resist taking more and more until, sometimes, she felt sick. That's why she was planning to get a lot of toffee rolls to stash away.

Monkeys lived everywhere in Shimla, above the large ridge in the bushy trees, and even on the rooftops of the shops in the marketplace. Some Indians called them sacred—but not Komal! She thought that monkeys were naughty and rude, climbing up on people and pretending to be innocent clowns!

Komal couldn't stand their pretend innocence, or their climbing skills, or how they acted like cute little rascals. Monkeys in those trees are always thinking up mischievous plans. Monkeys would scurry around to grab bits of food from the shoppers and the garbage on the trails. Yum! Just the perfect place for a monkey! Those clever animals could even ignore the noise of the shoppers in the marketplace and focus on making raids to and from the trees. They loved snacking on bananas and leftover food.

Komal walked along the old, rocky, black, shabby trail with Nakul, Tara, and Sohum.

"Let's walk down the more peaceful long way," said Sohum

happily.

"We don't have time!" answered Komal.

"We can take a shortcut through the alleys," Tara said. Finally, they stopped at the Mahajan store.

"Here at last!" Nakul said. "I can't wait to have my nut and fruit chocolate bar."

Once again, Komal imagined her everlasting stash of toffee rolls. Then Komal found her mouthwatering snack, chewy and sweet. Tara took some masala-spicy-chips, tangy and spicy, and Nakul and Sohum took nut and fruit chocolate bars that were creamy, chocolatey, nutty, and deliciously fruity.

"Let's sit on the bench to eat. I'm too hot and tired to keep walking," said Komal, for she had already eaten a few toffees and her belly ached with every step!

They rested on the stone bench by a huge tree and then resumed their walk.

As they walked homeward, a monkey poked his head out from a tree. He had just finished a banana, but that rascal monkey wanted MORE!

Hmm! he thought. *Something smells quite good.* He saw Komal with her huge bag of toffees and thought, *She has to share those toffees! I'll get her friends' snacks, too.*

As he watched Nakul, Sohum, Tara, and Komal with their food, again he jumped from the tree, quietly chattering, and crept up behind the four kids who were oblivious to the monkey's presence. The monkey made a quiet noise that sounded like "Arryoriy." Sohum's sharp ears caught the noise and he turned around.

"A MONKEY ROBBER!" he yelled. Tara, Komal, and Nakul spotted the monkey and screamed, "AHH! IT'S AFTER US! LET'S GO!"

The monkey let out a shrill cry. His naughty monkey friends jumped down from the tree. "*Shikanon!*" the monkey commanded, which meant, "Get their food."

The monkeys chased the children through the mall, past Jhakhu Hill, past the foothills of the Himalayas, past Summer Hill, to the Ridge, twisting and turning past Christ Church, with its plaques listing all the British soldiers who died in the wars.

On the children flew down the road, winding, twisting, turning, screaming, and running with the monkeys chasing them. They panted hard! The children felt as if their hearts were beating at six million beats a minute!

Suddenly, the first monkey grabbed one of Komal's braids and, with his other flexible paw, he caught hold of Komal's bag of toffee rolls.

"Let go!" Komal cried, tugging at the bag.

She started crying, not so much from sadness, but from rage. Blind with fury, she grasped the bag with all her might and tugged. The bag came loose, and Komal lost her balance and fell. Quickly, she got up and ran, clutching her candy, but the monkeys kept after her!

Soon Komal could see the old, familiar wooden bridge on the path ahead.

She yelled to the others, "Quick! Throw your snacks down off the bridge!"

Tara, Nakul and Sohum flung their snacks off the bridge. So did Komal. The monkeys dove down to grab the food. As he munched on the chewy, delicious, sweet toffee rolls under the bridge, the monkey leader thought, *Oh, what nice children! They did share, after all.*

When the four kids reached home, they all said in unison, "WE'RE NEVER GOING TO BUY SNACKS AGAIN!"

But as Komal took off her muddy boots and coat, she began to feel a little thankful to the monkeys. From the wild chase she had learned a lesson. What was it? Why, of course, NEVER TAKE TOO MUCH FOOD!!!

THE END

200

Jennifer Mazi mentored Kayla Davis through a revision focused on humor in Kayla's story, "Barker."

Dear Reader,

Before revision, Kayla Davis's hilarious and outlandish romp "Barker" was already funny. She has a knack for creating humor through dialogue, action and narration. But with humor, as Kayla reminds us, sometimes you have to push past the obvious things that we find funny in order to surprise us, too. That's how you make your reader laugh out loud.

How do you do this? Great question, and one that Kayla answered with banana peels and rubber floors. Play with surprising images and experiment with words. Consider using surprising contrasts with word choice to create additional humor. Online, there are lists of words that are funnier than others. For some reason, certain consonants are funnier than others, so you might have fun switching out words to choose the funniest options.

Also, look for areas where you may be telling your reader something is funny instead of showing them. Kayla went back through her story and found places where she used adverbs to tell us how Barker was feeling. She replaced them with physical action that gave us hilarious situations and mannerisms that caused Barker to leap off the page to tickle our funny bones.

Consider whether you can add more physical comedy anywhere in the story. You can either exaggerate what you have, or find other moments to include physical comedy, or both.

Finally, did your writing make YOU laugh out loud? If the answer is yes, there's a good chance your reader will be laughing, too.

Happy Writing,

Jennifer

Jennifer Mazi is a Writer of Many Things. She lives in Kansas City, MO, and is constantly on the prowl to find a Cloak of Invisibility. When she is not acting like a kid, she is making up stories for them, usually funny ones, sometimes involving talking planets.

Kayla Davis

Kayla Davis is ten years old and goes to La Entrada Middle School. Her favorite animal is a dog, so it is no wonder she wrote "Barker," a story starring one. She lives in Menlo Park, California, where she enjoys softball, swimming, reading, playing with her dog, Minnie, and joking around with her almost-eight-year-old sister, Lilah. Kayla's parents are Mrs. Karen Davis, and her very funny father, Mr. Eric Davis. When she grows up, Kayla would like to be a comedian.

Here are some of Kayla's thoughts on the writing and revision of "Barker."

What changes did you make during revision that made your story even funnier?

I really focused on showing, not telling, what was funny. Sometimes, this meant taking out a single word like *sleepily* and replacing it with a line or two to describe how Barker was acting during that time. This made some parts of my story fatter in some places, and then I had to work hard again to cut out some words in the end so my word count was smaller than it was when I started.

I also changed the names of the clowns from boring names like Matt to Fizzypaws and Bonkers! Bonkers is such a funny word and a great name for a clown. The clowns acted more like animals than the animals did, so this worked well.

We talked about narrative voice during the revision process, and whether changing this story to first person would make it funnier, but ultimately you wanted to stick with third person. Are you glad you did that?

Yes. Definitely. The best part of my story is the twist at the end that tells us who was really writing the story. That would have been lost if I had switched it to first person.

While your story is in third person, you still had to write this story as if you were a dog. Was that hard to do?

No. I studied my dog for a while and asked myself if I wanted Barker to act more like a dog, or more like a human. I decided that Barker had actual human thoughts, and many human characteristics, and I think that's what makes him so funny. I mean, a dog who signs autographs? That's hilarious!

You talk about how, in comedy, you have to push past the obvious to find a new way to tell a joke. What do you mean by that?

Take a banana peel for instance. That's funny. That's used a lot, though, the old "sliding on a banana peel" joke. I had to ask myself, how could I make that funnier? Then I came up with the idea of the rubber floor. So not only did the clown slip on the banana peel, but then he started bouncing around the room because the floors were rubber!

Any plans for a sequel?
Yep.

Barker

by
Kayla Davis

208

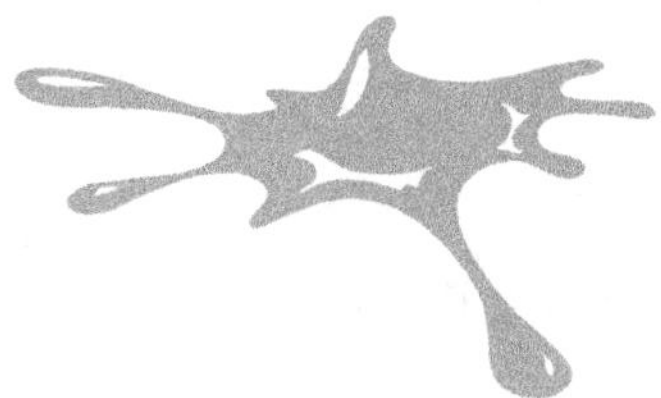

"Oh oh," thought Barker. "3, 2, 1—"

"Barker, Barker!" the crowds shouted. Barker walked outside. He yawned and stretched his paws. He almost fell back asleep, but he jerked himself out of his daze. He started to dip his paw in ink, and then put it on a piece of paper. Every morning at 6:00 am, he would start the day this way. "BARKER'S AUTOGRAPH - $5 APIECE" a sign read above his front door. There was always a clown collecting money. There were always many visitors. There was always around $500 in the collecting tin. And always, at 7:30 am, he would get ready for his 7:45 am show. The circus life was a tiring one, but a good one.

"Barker, it's almost time for your show," said the ringmaster. "You'd better be ready."

"Oh no!" said Barker frantically. "Where's my tie? Where's my toupee?!"

"What are you, a businessman?" jeered a clown.

"Yes, that's exactly what I'm supposed to be," snapped Barker.

"Five minutes 'til curtain!" said another clown.

"Thank you, five!" Barker shouted. He never set things out the night before, which was why he was always late for his act. When it was time, Barker started sweating like crazy and running about.

* * *

Barker excitedly entered the stage at 7:44 – a new record! He jumped up, wagged his tail, and yapped. Then he stopped. He didn't want the audience to think he was a common mutt when he entered. As he went through the doggy door to the stage, he looked around. So different, yet so familiar. The stage was set as a glass-sided office with a desk and a chair in it to go with his businessman attire.

"Well," he thought, "Showtime!" He ate a banana and threw it Stage Left, where his partner would come in.

"Where's my secretary?!" he shouted, and hopped on the chair.

"Right here!" said Bonkers, a clown, stepping through the door. Suddenly, he slipped on the banana peel and fell flat on his face. The crowd howled with laughter. He bounced up on the rubber floor and fell backwards. Soon, he was bouncing around the room.

"Come on and bounce over here so I can punish you for being so careless!" yelled Barker. The audience cheered and clapped as he jumped off the chair. That was a mistake, though, because he, too, bounced around the room. Up and down, this way and that, and off the stage, where he fell on the hardest pillow ever.

"OWWEEEEEEEEEEEEE!" Barker yelled in pain. Bonkers giggled and laughed. Then Bonkers rolled around hysterically on the floor.

"BONKERS!" Barker yelled. Bonkers ran out the door and into the clowns' barracks. Barker got up, sighed, and went to sit at his dressing room table. He would have chased after Bonkers, except that he didn't want to go into the clowns' barracks. The clowns would make fun of him, and besides, those barracks curtains just weren't his style.

He sipped a cup of coffee, while arguing with Fuzzypaws, who was insisting Barker's act was terrible. Barker didn't like Fuzzypaws, but he let him in his dressing room out of pure politeness. Also, the clowns made him do it.

Fuzzypaws was the circus cat. He did a "cute" act where all he did was lick his paws and purr. In the beginning, they had been friends. But that was when Barker was a puppy, and Fuzzypaws had tried to persuade him to join his "cute" act. Over the years, they had grown further apart because Barker was getting all the attention. They had then started a regular dog-cat relationship: cat insults dog, dog gets mad, they start to fight. They were about to start Round Two, when there was a knock at the door.

"Huh?" asked Barker, his jaws open, ready to bite Fuzzypaws. "Who is it? I'm not signing any autographs right now."

The mayor stuck his head in. "May I come in?" When Barker nodded, the mayor began his lecture.

"You're starting to get boring," he drawled. "Think up something new or I'll fire you."

"You can't fire him, though I'd like to see him go," said Fuzzypaws.

"You're not in charge of him."

"I am the mayor and I can do whatever I want. I am 'in charge' of the whole city!"

"I guess you're right," said Fuzzypaws. "Nice knowing you, Barker. Whoopee!"

"No, don't, Mr. Mayor," Barker begged. "This is my life!"

"No buts, Mr. Acaro."

Barker flinched. He hated people using his last name. Fuzzypaws looked at him and snickered.

"I'll kill you, cat," growled Barker, "if it's the last thing I do."

* * *

Now Barker needed to change his act, and Bonkers and the other clowns were talking.

"Maybe we could dye his fur green."

"Or we could shave him and make him sing opera."

"You will not!" Barker screamed. "I just need a new partner."

"How about Fuzzypaws?"

"NO!" Barker shouted, his paws crossed. Fuzzypaws looked at him, confused.

"Okay, then who?" the clowns inquired.

"I don't know, but it has to be a dog. I don't want a cat. Or another clown."

Now Bonkers looked confused.

They went to the animal shelter to find a dog. Barker reviewed the available dogs critically.

"No, not that one. I don't want him drooling on me. That one? He's a bulldog! That Chihuahua will just yap, yap, yap all day."

Suddenly they heard a voice.

"Please, let me out of here!" begged a small, spotted dalmatian that looked suspiciously familiar. Barker turned, surprised.

"MA!"

The dalmatian turned. "Why, you look just like my little pup Barker, except older," she exclaimed sadly.

"But Ma, I am your 'little pup Barker,' don't you remember me?"

She paused and squinted her eyes at him.

"Oh, Barker, it really is you! Look how big you've grown!" Barker disappeared in a flurry of Ma's hugs and licks.

* * *

Years ago, people had found Barker and his Ma living in an old box. When they crooned and talked baby to him because he was so small, Barker had gotten annoyed.

"I'm five years old. Don't talk to me like that," he responded.

"Shhh, Barker, don't talk," Ma cautioned. She knew that if people discovered he could talk, they would take him away, like they did with her sister. Yes, Barker had an aunt. She had been taken and tested on in a lab, and eventually died.

Unfortunately, Barker kept on gabbing. As Ma predicted, the people had taken him from her. But rather than taking him to a lab, as Ma assumed, the people took Barker to the circus, and Ma to the animal shelter.

Barker remembered being in a car, feeling scared and lonely, and thinking he would never see Ma again. When he arrived at the circus gates, the ringmaster was delighted, and Barker became part of the circus family. But he still missed his Ma. Now, reunited at last, he insisted they take Ma back to the circus.

* * *

Three days after their reunion, Barker sighed as he threw doggie sweaters and bones around a new bedroom set onstage. Hearing Ma advancing offstage, Barker quickly picked up a comic book and lay down in his doggie bed.

"Barker, your room is disgusting!" Ma exploded as she entered the stage, putting her paws on her hips. "Clean it up right now!" The audience giggled as she picked him up by the scruff of his neck.

"Uh, no. I don't really want to," Barker mumbled.

"What was that?" she narrowed her eyes at him so that all the audience could see.

The crowd laughed. Ma growled menacingly at him, then turned and gave the audience an exaggerated wink. The crowd howled, delighted. Barker sighed. He already missed being famous. Ma had taken all the attention. "But then again," he thought, "she deserves some credit."

Epilogue

Do you want to know what Barker did after Ma joined his act? He wrote a story. Do you want to know who wrote this story? Well, here's the autograph.

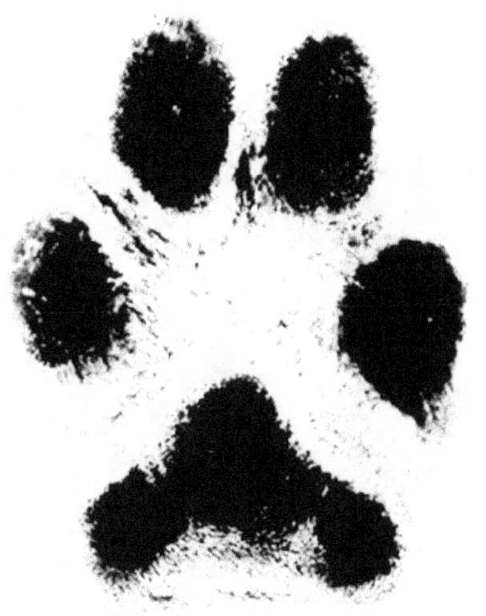

Need I say more?

Character Development

Andrew Steeves mentored Kevin Ma through a revision focused on character development in Kevin's story, "Nightmare."

Dear Reader,

Kevin came to me with a wonderfully creepy story about a professor plagued by nightmares. It was intense and frightening, but I wanted more than to be frightened. I wanted to be frightened for the professor, and so we decided to work on his development as a character.

A well-developed character is one of the most important thing your story can have. Settings can be enchanting, plots can twist and turn, but rich characters are at the beating heart of all good stories. We don't read *The Hunger Games* simply because of the dark cruel world that forces children into combat. We read it because we care about Katniss. We want to know what happens to her. We want to know whether she ends up with Gale or Peeta (Team Peeta for life!). The reason we care is because she's well developed. She's so rich and deep and interesting and complicated that we forget that she isn't real.

So, how do you make your character more developed? First, think about your character. Who is she? Where was she born? Did she go to school or not? Was her family rich or poor? Allow yourself to daydream about your character. What's her favorite color? Favorite food? You don't have to put the answers to these questions, but it's important that you the author knows the answers because you will know your character better.

Next, take your character out of your story and picture her in a different story. How would Katniss react in the world of Harry Potter? How would Harry react in Bella's vampire infested hometown? Again, this is just for you to think about, so you know how your character will react in any situation.

Now, put your character back in your story. How would she react to the things happening around her there? If you don't know the answer, then your character isn't acting because she wants to, but because the plot is making her. Pretend your characters are real, let them make their own choices, and they'll become real.

Finally, fill in some details from your character's history into the story. If something in the story reminds you of your character's history, let that bleed into the text. And if your character decides to do something different than you'd originally planned, don't be afraid to follow them. You might be surprised where you end up.

Write on,

Andrew

Andrew Steeves is a proud resident of Milwaukee, Wisconsin where he spends his time writing, telling stories, and spoiling his newborn daughter. He holds a B.A. in English from the University of Wisconsin-Milwaukee and an M.F.A. in Creative Writing from Hamline University. Andrew has published short fiction with UWM's undergraduate review *Furrow* and in *Undiscovered: Tales of Exploration, Adventure, and Excitement* from Hall Brothers Entertainment. In addition, Andrew is a winner of the 2013 Shabo Award for excellence in picture book writing.

Kevin Ma

Kevin is an 8th grader at Town School for Boys in San Francisco. He enjoys hanging out with friends, playing basketball, and video games. His favorite foods are burritos and fried chicken. He is a firm believer in the notion that duct tape can solve any problem in the world.

Here are some of Kevin's thoughts on the writing and revision of "Nightmare."

Why did you want to write a scary story?

It was actually a class assignment. You were given a choice of three sentences. Two of them were pretty weird, and one led you down a path of a scary story. So that's just what I wrote.

So you had those three sentences. One took you to a scary story, then you ran with it?

Yeah, I honestly made things up as I went along.

That was your first draft. Do you have a better idea of what the story is now that you've revised?

Definitely. The professor is more fleshed out, you know more about him. It's definitely a better story.

Did you learn anything new about your story during your revision?

> I learned about my character, I had to sort of make stuff up and figure him out more. In my first draft, I didn't really know who he was. It was just a scary story meant to scare you. There wasn't really a backstory.

Do you think the backstory makes it more scary? Less scary?

> Now that you know the character, you can care for him and relate to him, I feel like it makes the story more scary. It makes you think that maybe this could happen to you.

I gave you about three weeks to revise. Now be honest, there are no wrong answers, when did you start your revision?

> Maybe about the middle of the last week. I was procrastinating a lot because of exams. I did finish it on time though!
>
> The first day we had the interview I tried to do some revision, but I found I couldn't really think of anything because… I didn't know what to write. I had writer's block or something. Then exams came and I had to study for those.

Did having the deadline help?

> Yeah, I feel like I'm pretty good under pressure. If there hadn't been a deadline I probably would've waited longer.

Is this the first story you've written?

> No, I've written a bunch of stories, I just haven't submitted most of them.

Do you tend to write scarier stories?

I prefer to write fictional, non-scary stories. I'm not very good at scary stories because I can't write them at night.

Because you yourself get frightened?

Yeah.

Well that means you're good at writing scary stories if you're scared!

Yeah, I guess. I just prefer to write fictional stories of all kinds.

How do you come up with your ideas for your stories?

Well, for this one the first sentence helped. Then I just sort of sat there for twenty minutes. Then I started writing. I don't know what happened.

And do you have any specific writing habits? Does it help to write in a specific place, at a certain time of day? Can you just write anywhere?

I can pretty much write anywhere.

What did you get out of this story after revising? Did you learn anything? What was the experience like?

It was pretty fun. It was cool to realize that scary stories can be fun to write, even if they give you nightmares, but it was fun. I learned that your characters need to be detailed for the reader to care about them.

Did you get any nightmares from writing this story?

Maybe!

Nightmare

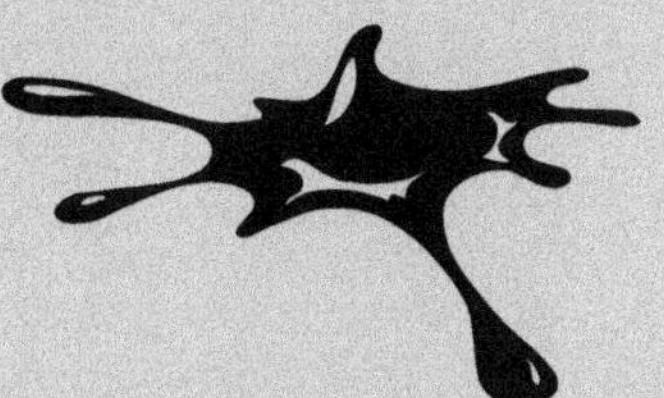

by

Kevin Ma

224

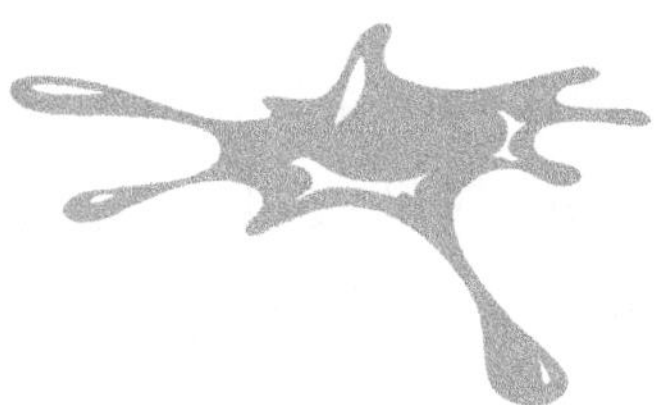

igid with fear, sitting up in bed, I stared helplessly as a face rose up in the moonlit window. When it stared at me with its bloodshot eyes, I tried to look away, but found myself paralyzed. My heart thumped as I whispered to myself,

"Don't move and it will go away. Don't move and it will go away."

The face twisted into a demented smile and slowly faded away into the darkness.

I gasped for air and opened my eyelids. Light flooded my vision. Shuddering, I realized that my body was covered in cold sweat. My eyes darted from side to side, scanning the white room for abnormalities. There weren't any.

"Everything is normal. It was just a dream."

I lay down in my bed and covered my sweaty face using my hands, and I tried desperately to remember when life was good. I tried to remember life before the nightmares came. That was my way of relaxing; it was how I recovered from the trauma I endured.

I was only a child when I realized that science was my passion, even though my village was poor and resources were scarce. Any other subject apart from science simply did not interest me. Eventually, all of my teachers, except one, gave up on me. I was labeled incompetent and useless by nearly everybody, including my own mother. My science teacher was the only one who believed in me. He became more than a teacher to me. I saw him as the father I never had. He became closer to me than even my mother.

Suddenly, my memory went blank, and I was forced to open my eyes.

Then, I heard a voice in the hallway. "Sir, he's awake," it said.

"Don't hurt me," I prayed. *"Please."*

The door flew open and the monsters came in. I tried desperately to look away, but I was paralyzed. I repeated to myself not to scream, but my mouth was open and I could feel the sound my own screaming in my chest. They pinned my arms down using their sharp claws and glared at me with their wicked, bloodshot eyes. They opened their mouths, showing their knifelike teeth, and lunged at me.

I forced my eyelids to shut. Even with closed eyes, I could still see the outlines of the monsters that tried to kill me.

"Just another dream," I told myself. I hoped it was true.

I used whatever strength I had left to think back. I remembered when I dreamed of going to college in the nearby city. I knew that I had little chance of making it, but I kept hope just in case. My science teacher visited the college every day during my final year of high school, trying to convince them that I would be successful. A day after I graduated, I was sent a letter of acceptance from the college. As always, my science teacher was proud of me. I even saw a glimmer of pride from my mother, who had long given up hope on me at that point. Above all, that was the first time that I was proud of myself.

When I opened my eyes again, the monsters were gone. My caregivers stood over me with worried looks in their eyes. I wondered whether or not they were truly able to be trusted, and my heart began to race again. I crawled into a fetal position and looked at each one of them, trying to determine if they were real or not.

"Professor, calm yourself," one of them breathed. "Calm yourself," another repeated.

"Calm yourself," they all said in unison.

I knew exactly what was going to happen, but I was still petrified as if it were my first nightmare.

Instantly, they morphed into monsters. Their faces were hideous and zombie-like. Their limbs became sharp spears. The fiends screeched a horrifying noise and lashed their limbs at me. Then, everything was bright.

My eyes were closed. I thought back, and remembered dropping out of college to pursue a career in science. Everyone thought that I had made the wrong decision, but I knew that it was right choice. My first paper was published into a world-renowned scientific journal. I continued to write and had much success. Colleges and the government began to provide me with plenty of money and equipment. Before long, my name was known across the country within the scientific community.

My eyelids opened. I was awake. I knew it this time. I looked up at my one caregiver. My chest was covered with small monitors, which were connected to a computer that monitored my heart rate.

"Professor," the caregiver said. His name was William. He was my favorite.

He would always listen to me when no one else wished to. "What happened in your dream?"

I proceeded to explain what I saw in my nightmare while William wrote every word I spoke in his notebook. When I began to say what happened in my hallucination, I felt a chill down my spine. I shook it off and finished my account.

"Professor, I have some bad news," he said quietly. "You had 87 nightmares last night, and 42 the night before that."

I looked up at him. He looked quite somber. There was some wetness in his eyes. He looked as if he was going to cry.

"Unfortunately, if you continue to have traumatic experiences at this rate," he paused. "You will not be able to live much longer."

"You have been my inspiration for all my life," William sighed. "You have made so many incredible discoveries. You have lived a life truly worth honoring."

He turned around and left my room, closing the door. Strangely, I was not shocked or unhappy to hear the information. Rather, I felt quite relaxed, and… happy. I sat up in my bed and looked out the window. I half expected the face to appear again, but it did not.

I leaned my head back and stared at the ceiling. I remembered when I was in the heyday of my career. Then, I found out that my old science teacher had been murdered. The news was broken to me by my mother. About a week later, she was killed as

228

well. I lost nearly all of the meaning in my life. I had nothing to live for, nobody left to impress. I fell into depression. My first nightmare was absolutely the most terrifying thing I had ever experienced. They were so lifelike, I almost couldn't tell the difference between a nightmare and reality. My nightmares became so frequent, and so traumatic, that I had a chance of dying every time I fell asleep. My condition was the first of its kind.

I laid down in my bed and closed my eyes. For the first time in 8 years, I slept without a single dream.

Resolving the Conflict

Kelly Smith mentored Sankalpa Guitam through a revision focused on resolving the conflict in Sankalpa's story, "Cheesy & Squeaky the Adventure Mice."

Dear Reader,

In Sankalpa's charming story about two inseparable mice setting forth on a whirlwind adventure, we chose to focus on resolving the conflict by providing the reader with a few more details so that the story ends logically, moving evenly from its exciting beginning to its unexpected and delightful ending.

Authors often struggle with how to write an ending, but your ending doesn't have to be perfect or even have the typical happy ending. You might just need to let the story naturally end. Just like the beginning of a story is when the conflict is introduced; the ending is the point when the natural flow of events reaches a resolution.

One way to do this is to reread your story and see if it ends when the struggles are over. Things can go on too long; there's always one more loose end to tie up or another character needing a happy ending. When writing your resolution, you can usually be fairly brief. The details must come from the plot, but not detract from the thing that makes the plot engaging: the conflict.

Alternatively, some stories end so neatly the reader rejects them. Endings that are cliché or just too simple may be unbelievable and seem out of sync with the rest of the story. When your plot begins and escalates in action and intensity, you create excitement and anticipation for your ending. If it appears too easy, obvious or silly, it may disappoint your readers and even

spoil their enjoyment of the whole story.

You should approach your rewrite as a precious opportunity to put those final touches on your story. This can help you make your characters even more endearing and will tell their story through a natural chain of events leading up to a satisfying and rewarding ending.

Happy Writing!

Kelly

Kelly Smith is an educator in a mixed-age, 4/5 classroom at an alternative school in Saratoga, CA. She is passionate about working with developing writers and instilling a lifelong love of the craft - even through the tough essay years! Kelly's a graduate of the Fine Arts Program at Montana State University. She lives with her husband and daughter halfway between the redwoods and the Pacific.

Sankalpa Guitam

Sankalpa can relate to mice really well. She is small, swift and sometimes shy, but very adventurous. She's in the 5th grade at Stevenson PACT Elementary. Sankalpa loves being outdoors - playing with friends, riding her bike, hiking and most of all seeing the beauty in nature.

Here are some of Sankalpa's thoughts on the writing and revision of "Cheesy & Squeaky the Adventure Mice."

How was your revision experience?

I normally hate revising but in school I know I have to; when I finish a story I just want to be done! This time, though, I thought it was very helpful. I made some important changes. I realized I had left out a BIG detail that would have made my story confusing to the reader. So I revised and was also able to make my story more adventurous and fun. It feels complete now.

You shared a lot of other great stories with me. How do you come up with your ideas?

I really don't know! They just come to me. Sometimes other books I read give me ideas. I really love to read!!

What are some of your favorite books?

I love reading about mysteries and adventures. I also really like series: Rick Riordin's *Heroes of Olympus*, books written by Roald Dahl, *Dear Dumb Diary* books, *Geronimo Stilton*, and *The Phantom Tollbooth*.

What are you writing next?

The third "Cheesy & Squeaky the Adventure Mice" story. I have finished writing the second one in the series. I am going to work on the third book. I want it to be a big series!

236

Cheesy & Squeaky

The Adventure Mice

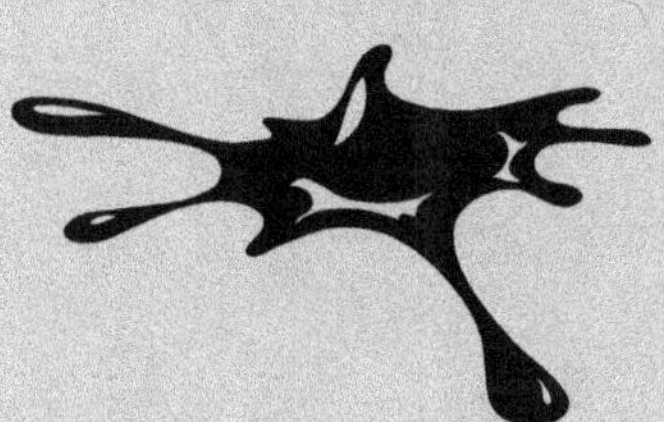

by

Sankalpa Guitam

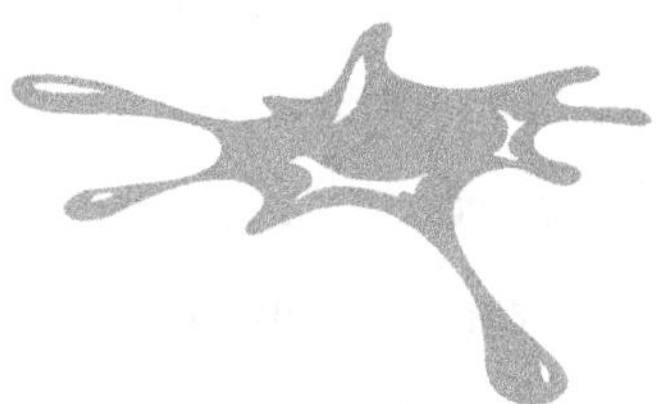

One nice and peaceful morning, Cheesy, the five-year-old mouse, started screaming. His mother, Swissy, came rushing into the room. His father, Cheddar, also had to drop the cup of tea that he was drinking because of the unbearable noise. Even his neighbors came rushing and knocked at the door. They all asked him this:

"WHY ARE YOU SCREAMING?!"

Then he started to cry. This was his way of getting sympathy and attention from all the mice.

Suddenly, all of the mice scurried away, as if they were following cheese, feeling really guilty for making a super adorable five-year-old mouse cry. After everyone left, Cheesy smirked as he went to his room. But his pride didn't last for long.

His parents stopped him as he made his way to the second story of the mouse hole. They had grown used to Cheesy's pitiful cry because they had lived with him for five years. They asked him why he had screamed so loudly. He was expecting them to yell at him, but instead they asked him softly. Before Cheesy could answer, Swissy had smelt something and realized that the cookies she was baking had started to smoke. So she scurried off to the kitchen.

Cheesy said to Cheddar, "I lost my star-shaped lollipop!!!" Cheddar understood immediately. Cheesy's star-shaped lollipop had been his most favorite thing in the world, since he got it when he was born. He spent time with it everywhere; dinner, bed, showers, even the amusement park where he almost lost it. Cheesy liked it even more than cheese, which was unbelievable for any mouse to accept. Suddenly, there was a knock on the door.

Cheesy opened it and saw Squeaky. She was his best friend ever. He even treated her like a sister. Cheesy and Squeaky stuck together like two magnets and never separated. Even Cheesy's lollipop didn't matter as much as Squeaky did to him. Squeaky was his neighbor, so she would always call Cheesy over for a playdate at her house. Even when Squeaky went to Switzerland, she brought Cheesy and his family.

Squeaky had allergies to dairy products and many mice would make fun of her because she couldn't eat cheese. But she didn't care. Squeaky was strong and brave. She and Cheesy were like twins. Their minds thought very alike. They both were born in November. Cheesy was born on November 7 and Squeaky was born on November 21.

Cheesy would carry a star-shaped lollipop and Squeaky would carry a heart-shaped lollipop. The star-shaped lollipop was hard, tasty, and blue. The heart-shaped lollipop was hard, tasty, and pink.

Squeaky said that she had come because she heard Cheesy screaming so loudly that she woke up thinking it was her alarm clock. But when she saw all of her neighbor friends rushing towards Cheesy's house, she decided to come over to see what the problem was. Once she asked Cheesy why he was crying, Cheesy screamed again but softer so that no other mouse in a different mouse hole could hear him. He said this,

"MY STAR-SHAPED LOLLIPOP IS MISSING, HAVE YOU SEEN IT? I DOUBT THAT YOU HAVE!"

Squeaky said in a nice tone that she hadn't. Squeaky always remained calm. Cheesy, on the other hand, would always freak out. This was their only difference in personality. Squeaky said that she had lost her heart-shaped lollipop too. Then Cheesy had an idea. So did Squeaky. They both had the same idea.

They were the richest animals in the whole world, so they bought a private jet just for themselves. This was when their journey to find the star-and heart-shaped lollipops began.

They went across America, their home country, and saw the Statue of Liberty. Then they went to Africa and saw the desert land full of animals, where they were chased by a hyena. After that, they went to India and saw the Taj Mahal. While they were there, a peacock tried to eat them. Next, they went to China and saw the Great Wall of China. In China, they nearly got trampled by a parading Chinese dragon. Together, they went to Canada, Brazil, Antarctica, Europe, Russia, Japan, and Australia. Still, they couldn't find the star-and heart-shaped lollipops. Finally exhausted, they came back home. With frowns on their faces, they told both of their moms about what they had done.

Their moms laughed and said that they had seen Cheesy and Squeaky eating their lollipops in their sleep. Cheesy and Squeaky were happy. They had planned to wait to eat their lollipops the next morning, as it was five years and three days since they got their lollipops. The reason why it was five years and three days was because Squeaky's birthday (the 21st) divided by Cheesy's birthday (the 7th) equals three, the day that they would eat the lollipops.

But instead they had gotten too tempted in their sleep and ate it. Overall, they did have a great adventure, just the start of many more to come.

THE END

Tightening the Plot

Andrew Avallone mentored Shaheen Cullen-Baratloo through a revision focused on tightening the plot in Shaheen's story, "The Dark Side of Matter."

Dear Reader,

For "The Dark Side of Matter," I had Shaheen focus on making the story more succinct. The original version of his story was well over twenty pages, and he needed it to be less than ten in order for it to be included in this anthology. In order to accomplish this, I suggested he focus on tightening up the plot—remove any portion of the story that doesn't aid the reader in understanding the main characters or drive along the plot—as well as play with the language and revisit his conclusion. Essentially, look over all parts of the story and make sure it is all centered on the same goal; in this case, that goal was emphasizing what finding a home with Timothy meant for Matt. Matt had been floating aimlessly in space without any guidance or direction, but now had a place to call his own with people who cared about him.

Shaheen first removed parts of the story he deemed unnecessary, and then looked over his conclusion. I guided Shaheen towards a clearer conclusion. Like many writers, Shaheen viewed his conclusion as obvious ("Of course Matt did those things on purpose!), yet that was not my impression. Students often need prodding to help them realize readers do not have a window into their minds, and they need to be as clear and descriptive as possible.

When Shaheen and I reviewed his second version, I was really impressed by what was in front of me. It still had the humor and fun that makes "The Dark Side of Matter" stand out, but was tidy and concise. The great

part of this story is that it is written by a kid who may not even realize how poignant his story really is: it captures the essence of belonging and the safety in stability, all through the tale of a blob and a boy.

Write on,

Andrew

Andrew Avallone first discovered his love of writing thanks to his fifth-grade teacher, who told him she planned on reading one of his novels at the beach one day. He graduated from UC Santa Cruz with a degree in History, and spent the last two years as a fifth-grade assistant teacher at The Phillips Brooks School in Menlo Park. He is now a sixth-grade teacher at The American School of Quito, in Ecuador.

Shaheen Cullen-Baratloo

Shaheen is a bright-eyed, charismatic seventh grader who is fascinated by comic books, matter, and video games. He once got his finger stuck in a hose as a child, and is enthralled by physics. Shaheen's interest in writing began when he was inspired to write a fantasy epic involving evil kings and shacks that sell weapons to him and his friends. He likes creating characters that are different from how he acts in real life, which is how the rebellious, mischievous Matt was created.

Here are some of Shaheen's thoughts on the writing and revision of "The Dark Side of Matter."

Why do you enjoy writing?

I enjoy giving my story a voice, and I like making my writing pieces funny.

Where do you like to write?

I like to write on my computer at a desk at my house.

How do you come up with your ideas?

I usually just sit at my computer and see where my writing goes.

Do you ever feel blocked? What do you do?

Yes, and if I do, I take a break and come back to it later.

Who do you enjoy sharing your stories with?

My mom.

Are you working on a new story?

Not currently. Maybe four or five for fun outside of school. I began writing for fun because of interest in medieval weaponry, so I created a story about my friends in a fantastical setting with evil kings and shacks that sell weapons.

Where did the idea for "The Dark Side of Matter" come from?

At school, I did a report on anti-matter, and I am really interested in physics, so the next step was to explore normal matter. I tried to find a way for the dark matter to manifest itself, so I went with a blob.

What is your favorite thing about Matt?

He is silly and is a rascal. I liked making him talk in slang and be really bro-y.

How was the revision process for you? What was difficult?

Finding time was really difficult because of school winding down. Once I received the letter, I sat down and did it. I wrote the story a long time ago and considered submitting it, but just let it sit for a while. Then, I finally submitted it and Young Inklings emailed that I had won.

What is your family like?

I'm an only child. It can get kind of boring, but I don't have to worry about siblings and I have a ton of friends in the neighborhood. I like to play video games, play Nerf wars, and Attaktix. I like reading comic books. My favorite comic book character is The Punisher or Juggernaut. My dad is a software engineer, and my mom does something with data for a testing company.

What grade are you in? What is your favorite thing about school?

I'm in seventh grade. My favorite subject is math. I'm also really interested in physics. I watch *NOVA* and other science shows. My cousin has a degree in physics.

What is one thing not many people know about you?

When I was little, I was obsessed with sprinklers and got my finger stuck in a hose and the fire department had to come saw it out. Once, I got stuck in Canada at Niagara Falls by going through a revolving door that said "Do Not Enter" and my dad had to come rescue me by going through immigration to get me.

What is your favorite book?

Eragon, because it has a lot of medieval fantasy, dragons and kings.

The Dark Side of Matter

by Shaheen Cullen-Baratloo

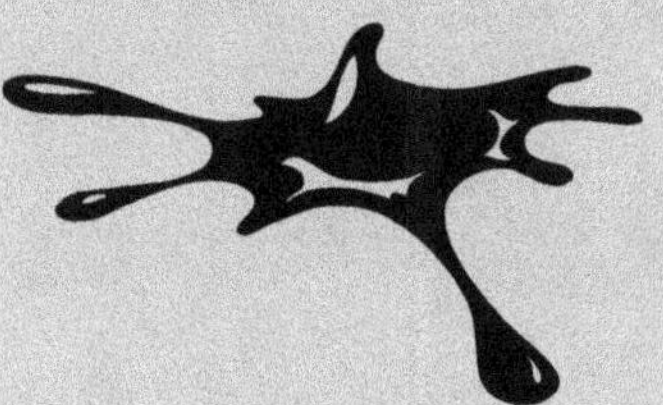

In the isolated universe of dark matter, everything was normal. Dark matter planets orbited around dark matter stars, and dark matter moons circled the dark matter planets. But somewhere in the dark matter universe, a random asteroid collision created a small black blob, about the size of a soccer ball. It was Matt, the first sentient creature made out of dark matter. Somehow, however, he could see normal matter.

* * *

Dude, this is, like, so lame, Matt thought to himself. He was floating through space, with nothing to do. Eventually, he saw a planet in the distance, all nice and red. He "swam" towards it and landed with a puff of dust. He formed himself into two legs and started walking around. Nothing, nothing, more nothing, a rock, more nothing, more rocks, nothing, nothing, NOTHING! There was no visible life on the planet. He pushed off and swam through space, towards another planet, which turned out to be lifeless, like the hundreds of thousands of planets which came after that one. But, he found a small blue and green planet, which happened to be more interesting.

* * *

Matt:

Dude, I totally hope this planet has life, I think, as I plummet towards a small planet. I imagine what the life forms might look like, but I can't, not having seen any livin' things before. 'Sides me, natch. Eventually, I crash on some sort of black thingymahoodle. Oozing around, I try to find something that moves.

In the distance I see some sorta red thing with a bunch of lights at the front and glass stinkin' everywhere. It has some black round things at the bottom. I stick out a gooey appendage, and try to get the thing's attention, but heck no. It just keeps on going, and passes over me. I just split around the black things, though, so no harm done. I see another one of those things, but this time it is mostly gray. It runs over me again. Geez, how much respect does a blob get these days?

Then I see something different: some sorta thing, completely un-blobby, standing on two blue appendages, with a red part on top of them. Out of the red part are two more appendages, which flop around. On top of the red part is a round thing that has a ton of black lines at the top. He uses the blue appendages to move around.

I wave at him.

The creature looks at me and starts babbling.

"Whoa. What the heck are you? An outer space blob? Wow! Just like my favorite video game character, Zac! Except that he's man-made. This is awesome! I can show all my friends, show astronauts, ask him about space—WOW! I mean, he's complete with everything! He can form appendages with his arms! He can make a mouth to absorb things! Just like in science class. What was it called? Phagocytosis? I don't know. I mean, groovy! AND HE'S ALL BLACK! Like space."

I don't know how, but for some reason I can understand him. I answer him.

"'Sup, dude."

"Wait, what?"

"'Suuuup…Duuuude."

"You came all the way from wherever you came from to say, 'Sup, dude?'"

"Uhmmm…well…er…" I don't know what to say. This is kinda lame. I ask him how he is doing, and I get this?

"Do you have a name?"

He draws me out of my thoughts. "Of course I have a name, nimrod! Why wouldn't I? You are talking to Matt, bro!"

The thingy looks at me funny. I look at him funny back.

"Where are you from?" he asks me.

"I am made of matter, and I don't know how, but I got created and sent through the dark matter universe."

"This isn't the dark matter universe." The creature seems puzzled.

"What do you mean? Of course it is!"

"Oh, I get it. Us humans call your universe dark matter, and you blobs call our universe dark matter."

So this thing is a "human."

"One thing, bro; I'm the only living thing made of dark matter."

"Ah," the human says quietly.

"So um-"

"Look out! Move!"

I don't know why the creature thingy is yelling at me. A second later, I split in half, as one of those colorful things with black parts at the bottom passes over me.

"Cars don't hurt you?" the human says in astonishment.

"Car? What's a car?"

"The thing that ran over you."

I look at him, trying to see if he is joking. "Why would they hurt me?"

The thing doesn't say anything. Who cares? Aw geez, I forgot about his name!

"What's your name, kid?"

"There's another car—never mind. I'm Timothy." Another of those "cars" runs over me. "Oh, I get it! You are a blob, so nothing can hurt you!"

"I guess so," I say. "I was floating through not-your matter space for most of my life, so I don't know, really."

"'Kay. I have to go. See ya." Timothy turns to go. He turns back around. "Wait. Matt, do you feel like coming home with me?"

"What? Sure!" Finally, I, a blob of dark matter, am gonna go to some living thing's house! Whoopee! I hope it has lots of good food.

"Follow me." Timothy pulls me out of my daydream and beckons for me to follow. I ooze along behind him.

I get a ton of rocks mixed in with my goo as I slide along, so I decide to try the human approach to moving. I form myself into two appendages, vaguely like the bottom of Timothy's body, and move one appendage, then the other, and I find it hard to balance, so I go back to oozing.

Eventually we get to some sort of giant white thing, with some glass panels here and there. It looks pretty boss. The top is slanted, and it has a tower made of bricks coming out of the top. The rest is like a rectangle. This seems kinda, like, boring. I probably wouldn't want to live there. But then again, I have no idea what it's like in there. So I'll judge later.

There is a red wooden rectangle, and Timothy pulls it out, so that there is a hole to get into the giant white thingy. It, like, looks really cool.

"Matt, you can't make a sound."

"What?" I feel, like, so confused. It is just so weird.

"Then my mom will see you. And she won't like that."

I roll my eyes. This is so, like, stupid. "So what if she hates me?"

"She'll kick you out of the house!"

"Then keep me. She isn't the boss of you."

"Umm...Yes she is."

Now I understand, and I don't even respond, hoping that his mom, is, like, two bazillion miles away.

He takes me up a ramp with lots of bump things. I don't know why the bump thingies are there; wouldn't it be easier to ooze up it without bump things? Whatevs. Eventually, he reaches a flat place, and I see a ton of those wooden rectangle things. He swings one in, and we enter the room. He closes the wood thingy.

"What is that wood thingy called?"

Timothy sighs. "A door."

"What about that thingy?" I stick out a blobby appendage and touch the big round thing at the top of his body.

"A head."

Then we launch into a conversation where he tells me, like, every word that I need to know, from computer to book to pizza to tree to eye to video game to sleep. Yeah, sleep is cool.

* * *

Matt:

"Timothy, lunch time!" Timothy's mom pops her head in through the door.

I wave at her, and she recoils, her eyebrows drawing together. She's about to start screaming when Timothy cuts her off.

"Chill. Please. WAIT! I can explain…"

"What on Earth is that?"

"I'm not from Earth—" I begin, before Timothy shoves me. I close my mouth. Or at least what approximates to my mouth.

"He's a blob from outer space. Can we keep him, please?"

His mom doesn't know what to say. "Well, I don't know, maybe…"

"Please?"

"Let's just see how he is for a bit. Then we'll decide."

Satisfied with this answer, Timothy drags me downstairs for lunch.

On the table, I see some pizza. I slingshot off the railings on the stairs, and land in a chair. A few tiny blobs of me fall off, but I bounce them up and they recombine with my body. Timothy takes the seat in front of me.

"Chow down, Matt!"

I open up a hole in myself, like a mouth, I guess, and gobble up some pizza.

"Wow, dude, so boss! This is so sick, bro! Can we have pizza every day? I want more!"

Timothy glares at me, and I shut up and gobble my pizza. Oooh... the, like, cheesy, gooey, tomatoey, bready goodness.... This is total heaven! Oh man, sooooooo good...

"Dude. I. LOVE. PIZZA!"

Timothy hushes me. "Sshhh. My mom will get ticked off if she hears you yelling."

"Okay, gee whiz."

Timothy mutters something, but I don't hear the dude 'cause I'm, like, busy up here in heaven. Pizza, pizza, pizza, more pizza, more pizza pizza pizza. Oh, and did I mention pizza?

The two of us walk up to Timothy's room. Or, at least, Timothy does. I ooze. We kill a few hours, not doing anything worthwhile. Before long, it's dinner time! I wonder if we're gonna munch on more pizza! I have to admit I'm kinda addicted. Ooooh, the cheesy goodness...This world that I've landed in... it's so... pizza-y. Stop thinking about pizza... no... but it's so good...

"We gotta go munch, blobface!"

"Oh, great."

Timothy ignores me. "C'mon. I have to go to school tomorrow."

"Oh, right. You told me about school. Is it fun?"

"NO! I hate it."

"Can I come with you?"

"We'll see."

Timothy's mom says "Dinner!"

"I don't smell pizza."

Timothy glares at me. "WE...ARE...NOT...HAVING... PIZZA...EVERY...DAY! We are having steak. If you don't like that, you can go hungry."

"'Kay."

We go in, and I see some steak in a few plates, and suddenly I remember Timothy's mom's conditions for me staying. So I try to behave and eat neatly, even though it's hard (yes, Timothy did tell me about manners). After we finish, we go upstairs, and Timothy gets ready for bed, and makes me a bed out of some clothes and towels. I can sleep on anything. Nothing really happens. We just go to bed, and Timothy has a nice sleep. I'm busy thinking about pizza.

* * *

Timothy:

I wake up, not looking forward to a day of school.

"Ugh..." I say, rubbing my eyes.

Then I rub them again. No, this is really happening...

"Oh, no," I say. "Matt, you idiot..."

I rest my head on my hand. He spent the entire night messing up my toys... taking apart my LEGO, playing on my phone, throwing around my action figures...

"At nighttime, you're supposed to sleep, or at least stay in bed! Don't mess up my stuff!"

My mom comes in. "Timothy, you have—Did a tornado hit your room last night?"

"No, not a tornado, the next best thing... Matt!"

"Sorry," Matt says sheepishly.

"You two will have to clean this up after school."

I glare at Matt.

I get ready for school, listening to Matt complain about how breakfast is "Bagels and eggs, not pizza," and brush my teeth, and pack my lunch and backpack. Then comes the problem of what to do with Matt.

"Hey Matt, do you want me to show you to the class? Or do you wanna hide?"

"Don't care."

So we are in the car, in the back, with Matt rooting around in my backpack and lunchbox, and me thinking about what to do with Matt.

"Can I eat your chips?"

"What—NO WAY!"

"Too late."

I snatch the lunchbox and backpack from him.

"No more touching my stuff!"

Matt starts fiddling with the window. I am going insane.

"Stop it! Just sit still, or my mom will kick you out!"

He finally sits still.

After a century, we get to school. I tell Matt that I am going to show him to the class, then put him in my cubby. We get to school, and I walk down the hallways to my classroom, with Matt in my arms. Next to the door, I put my backpack and lunchbox in my cubby, and carry Matt into my classroom. I tell my teacher, Mr. Smith, that I found this outer space blob named Matt, and I asked him if I could show Matt to the class.

"Hi, Mr. Smith!" Matt says, waving an appendage.

"Get out of here, Timothy. That blob is a fake, and you know it. Stop wasting my time."

"But I can—"

"PUT YOUR TOY AWAY, OR I'LL TAKE IT FROM YOU!" Matt seethes.

"That's not very nice, you jerk. I'm 100% real, not bogus at all. Bro, go insult someone else for no reason, not me. I haven't done nothin'."

"Oh, no…" I whisper for the second time that day.

Mr. Smith hands me a detention slip. "Go put it outside, now, or I'll send you to Mrs. Jones's office.

"Shut up," I hiss at Matt.

Once we're outside, I tell Matt that I'm going to be in class the whole day, and he needs to be quiet. I give him some action figures: Spider-Man, Doctor Octopus, Iron Man, and Backlash.

"Fine, I'll just sit here and be quiet," Matt pouts.

"'Kay, thanks." I walk back into class.

"Hello, class. Today you will be doing some grammar worksheets. We will learn how to use semicolons, and…"

* * *

Timothy:

After our grammar worksheets, the boredom continues.

260

"Today we will learn about the order of operations, and we will apply…"

I stop listening. I hope Matt is still in his cubby, playing with those action figures. But oh, no…what if he broke the action figures… Oh NO! Today is pizza day! What if he attacks the lunch lady? That would be bad.

"Timothy, would you mind doing this problem here on the board?"

I look up, and see a giant math problem, filled with division and multiplication and addition and exponents. That's when I hear the scream.

I look into the hall, past the door, and see a lunch lady carrying pizza boxes, running, and behind her… MATT! He's chucking the action figures I gave him at the lunch lady, trying to get her to give him the pizza.

"GET BACK IN YOUR HOLE!" I yell at him.

"Excuse me?" Mr. Smith says, towering over me. "Did I hear you correctly?"

"I'm sorry, I was yelling at my blob."

"ENOUGH WITH YOUR BLOB! GO SEE MRS. JONES!"

"But—"

"GO! NOW!"

I trudge towards the door. I turn left, then when Mr. Smith can't see me any more, I bolt towards the lunch lady and Matt.

"Get back here!" I yell at Matt. The lunch lady and Matt have a huge head start, but I try to catch up. They round a corner, and disappear from my sight. A little while later, when I round the same corner, I see the lunch lady faceplanted on the tiled floor, and pizza all over the walls and ceiling of the hall. And who is in the middle of this? Matt, with pizza all over him, burping.

"MATT!" I yell.

"What?"

"You have got to be kidding me."

"What?"

"I TOLD YOU TO STAY IN THE CUBBY, AND WHAT DO YOU DO? AMBUSH THE LUNCH LADY!"

"What happened here?"

I jump and turn around. "Um, well. I…don't know, really. Behind my back, I motion for Matt to hide under the lunch lady. He obliges, for once.

"Well, go find the nurse!"

"Okay." I dash off, and hiss at Matt, "Split yourself into tiny pieces, and DON'T MOVE!"

"Yes, sir," Matt says sarcastically, then splits himself. That's a new record, listening to me twice in one day!

I dash back a minute later with the nurse, only to find Mrs. Jones passed out.

"Oh, jeez—"

Whump!

I turn around. The nurse is on her back, her arms flailed out.

I turn on Matt, but can't find him. Then I see him on the roof, making faces at the nurse.

I'm about to kill him, when - Rinnnnnnggggg! The recess bell! I make a break for it. I finally slow down when I get to the field. I see Matt behind me, looking quite pleased with himself.

* * *

Matt:

"YOU CAN'T DO THIS! MY MOM WILL KILL ME, AND SO WILL THE PRINCIPAL! Blah, blah, blah, blah..." Timothy is yelling at me. I think.

Ooh, the pizza was so good! Bro, the lunch lady was so funny! She was like "EEK!" and I was like "PIZZA!" and she was like "blargh."

"Are you listening? Matt, you can't do this, ever again!"

"Ya, sure, whatevs, sure, fine, sorry, kay..."

I mean, dude, Timothy doesn't need to be blabbing his brains out. C'mon, bro, just live and let live. But I guess he has a point.

"Okay, I'll just sit in the cubby..."

"Thank you."

The rest of the day is boring. I just sit in Timothy's cubby, trying to not die of boredom. After school, Timothy and I just drive home, and he does his homework. Not very interesting. Except one thing.

"Matt, we have to clean my room, thanks to you!"

"Sorry." What's the big deal about room cleaning, anyway?

* * *

Matt:

The next day, Timothy lets me use a phone at school, so I behave. I spend the entire day playing a Kirby game. He's like me, a little blobby thing who likes to swallow stuff. After school, we go downtown.

"So where are we going again?"

"The toy shop, and a special surprise for dinner."

"'Kay."

"Now you boys be good," Matt's mom says as she drops us off. "I have to do some shopping, so I'll meet you at the place."

"Okay," Timothy responds.

* * *

Timothy:

Matt and I walk into the toy shop. I yank open the door, and we walk in. I wonder what kinds of things Matt would like.

"Hey, Matt, what kinds of toys do ya like? Action figures, LEGO, foam guns, robots, card games?"

No response. Oh, no!

I look around, only to find Matt has run away somewhere. And people are screaming and running around and bumping into things.

I search the store, down every aisle. No Matt. Then suddenly, I see him, with a ton of open science experiment kits.

"'Sup, Timothy. Do you know where I could get water?"

"YOU'RE NOT SUPPOSED TO OPEN THE THINGS HERE!"

Matt disappears again. I see him running off to the bathrooms. I chase after him. He hops into a sink in the women's bathroom, and starts mixing something. A moment later, I feel something gooey stick to my face.

"How do ya like my new goo? Made it myself."

I peel the stuff off, only to see that Matt has more in his blobby appendages. He chucks it around, knocking over displays and hitting people.

The owner comes over. "I'm afraid I'm going to—AAAAHHH!"

She breaks off when she sees Matt, and runs. Matt chases her, pelting her with goo.

"Get back here!" I yell, but he's already too far away. I chase after him, and I find him with a Nerf gun, firing at random people and things.

"These toy stores are fun! They have so many things to do!"

"You aren't supposed to…"

He runs away again.

Tinkle! Smash! Crack!

I hear windows breaking. I sprint towards the sound. I see Matt chucking a variety of balls at a window.

"This is so beast, man. Like, there are so many things to do here! Kids must have a blast when they go to a toy store!"

Then he runs away again.

I follow, but I lose him. I sprint around, checking all of the aisles. I skid into one, and see him at the end. I sprint towards him, but suddenly, I slip and fall on a ton of LEGO bricks! He's opened most of the sets, and is throwing LEGOs everywhere.

"Owwww…" I moan.

"Oh, sorry. Wanna come and join me? We can throw these block things around!"

"You aren't supposed to open these things in the store! And don't tell Mom about anything that happened in here. Say that we just didn't want to buy anything."

"Oh. Dude, but that's, like, so lame. Not groovy at all. But whatevs. Sorry, bro."

"And when we leave, be QUIET!"

"Sure, dude."

We're gonna have dinner at the pizza place. I hope Matt doesn't trash the place and run around eating everybody's pizza. That would be awful.

"So where are we going next?"

"A pizza place! Especially for you."

No response. I look at him. He has a glazed smile on his face and he is oozing along, in a trance. When we arrive at Joe's Pizza, Matt just walks in happily.

"Wait, don't go in! We have to wait for my mom!" He just turns around. In the distance, I see my mom. It takes forever, but she gets here, and we order our pizza. Matt, surprisingly, just sits quietly. When the pizza comes, he snaps out of it.

"PIZZA!"

He wolfs down his pizza, mine, and my moms, and leaps over the chair onto another table.

"What is he doing?" my mom asks.

I don't answer, I just run to chase Matt and his trail of pizza destruction.

People are running around and panicking. I see Matt gobbling a large veggie delite pizza. I jump on him.

"You can't eat everyone's pizza!"

"But dude, I was, like, hungry!" Matt struggles in my arms.

"You could have ordered more for yourself, but you CAN'T EAT OTHER PEOPLE'S PIZZA!"

"Gee whiz, man, you act like I committed some crime."

I carry Matt back to the table. My mom grabs my arm and drags me and Matt to the car. "Forget ice cream, we're having dinner at home. And Matt will have to go."

"What? No! Just one day! Please!"

I look over at Matt, who is just sulking in the car seat. He stays silent. He expands all over the seat, then contracts with a sucking sound. He expands again. It's almost like he's sighing, over and over.

"Please can he stay? He'll prove to you that he's good! Right, Matt?"

"Yeah, sure," he grumbles.

My mom turns around. She looks me in the eye. "He can stay, but only one day. After that—"

Ring ring ring! Ring ring ring!

My mom picks up her phone. After a long and boring conversation with Dad about roasted potatoes, she notices that her phone has low battery. She reaches into her handbag and grabs a car charger and goes to plug it in. I see some sort of tiny black thing fly across the car, landing on the charger. Nah, I must be going crazy. Right after, she drops it down the side of her seat!

"AARGH! STUPID CHARGER!"

She reaches down the seat, but she can't pick it up. "Dah! Now my phone will die, and I can't call your dad if something comes up!"

"I'll get it."

I turn around, surprised. Matt oozes out of his seat, and then slithers down into the crack.

"Found it." From the side of the chair, a white thing pops out. Mom grabs it.

"Thanks, Matt." She looks thoughtful.

For the rest of the trip, we sit in stony silence. Eventually, we pull up in our driveway. We all trudge out, and Matt just follows me, quietly, without any of his usual bounce. My mom slips on a black spot and her keys and bag go flying towards a small bush.

"Whoa, Mom, are you okay?"

"Yeah, I'm fine." She goes and grabs her bag, and frantically searches for her keys. "My keys! Where are... Timothy, we might be locked—"

Matt pops out of the bush. "Got 'em."

"Thanks." My mom breathes a sigh of relief. When we go in, my mom just cooks a simple egg and toast dinner. We eat silently, and after that, everyone is exhausted and we crash in bed.

The next morning, we are all feeling better, except for Matt. I can't blame the soon-to-be homeless blob. Although school isn't exactly something to be excited about, I am feeling okay. As we eat our breakfast of cereal and fruit, we hear a crash from the living room. Me and Matt ignore it, but mom goes to investigate.

"Our wedding picture! It fell behind the sofa!"

I rush into the living room, to see my mom trying to move the heavy sofa. "Timothy, help me!"

We both try to move it, but to no avail. The sofa is heavy, and neither of us is strong enough to move it.

Mom collapses onto the sofa. "That picture was from our wedding..." she groans. "I've lost most of the other ones." As she talks, I notice a faint black mark on the wall. I'm beginning to see what blob-for-brains is doing...

"We can always get it later, with dad or something..." I try to comfort her.

"Dad's not strong enough! We'll need to hire people, and that would be expensive."

"Why don't you try reaching down the sofa?"

"Already tried that. Even with a grabber, the back is too tall."

Suddenly the picture pops out from the top of the sofa, followed by a very depressed blob.

"Matt!" my mom yells. "You got it!"

"Yeah."

"Thank you so much!"

"Mmmm."

Mom looks at Matt approvingly. Maybe he will be allowed to stay! The li'l rascal. I don't wanna jinx it, though.

At school today, Matt just droops in his cubby. He doesn't cause any trouble, and doesn't do anything. No action figures, no video games, nothing. I mean, this is weird for him.

After we get home, we just go up to my room. Matt sits there, depressed, and I play on my phone. My mom comes into my room suddenly.

"Get ready, we're going out for dinner to a pasta place."

I like pasta! "Oooh, cool!"

Matt doesn't say anything.

We go out to Pasta Land, my favorite pasta place. But still nothing from Matt. He doesn't even order his own food. I have to order it for him. When it comes, he just quietly eats it. No "Why can't we have pizza?" No "Dude, this is lame. I want pizza." Nothing! I'm starting to worry. The check comes, and suddenly Mom freaks out.

"Ohmygosh! I lost my wallet behind the chair! Ahh! My driver's license, my debit card, my credit card... My money... Eeeeek! Argh! Ack! Oh no! No, no, no, no, no..."

I go over to help her. She shows me where it fell: in a small hole behind the seat. I can stick my hand in the hole, but I can only barely brush against the wallet. It seems strangely sticky.

My mom whispers in my ear, "And I just went to the bank today to get cash."

Oh, no. This is bad. Now the restaurant people will get mad at my mom for not paying. But then Matt pops out with the wallet.

"Yay!" My mom screams. "Thank you, Matt!"

For the first time in a while, she smiles. I can't dare to hope…

She pays for the dinner, and the rest of the evening is uneventful. We go home, and just hang around. While I'm reading my book, my mom comes into my room.

"I've been thinking."

"Uhhhhh…Okay…" I want to make a sarcastic comment, but if she's gonna say what I think she's gonna say, that would be a bad idea. I quickly look around for Matt, but he's nowhere to be found.

"Matt can stay."

A small black blob drops onto her head. "Groovy, dude!"

"Matt, you idiot!" I am horrified.

"It's fine," my mom laughs. Then the blob and I follow suit.

* * *

Timothy:

When my mom finally leaves, I confront Matt, realizing something.

"All those 'incidents' were too coincidental. Not to mention the black marks everywhere. Are you sure they were natural?"

"Uhhhh…"

"You made her drop the things, didn't you?"

Matt grins. "Urm… possibly?"

"You bonehead! Er, goohead!" I crack up even harder. I seem to have picked up a very defiant blob.

"Sorry. You can't blame me for being slippery!"

"Yeah, but… Oh, whatever." I jump onto my bed and laugh. I have to admit, I'm glad he stayed. Even if it was through trickery, evil, cunning, and deceit. I grin to myself.

272

Creating a Satisfying Ending

I.J. Austrian mentored Joseph Brentjens through a revision focused on creating a satisfying ending in Joseph's story, "The End of the Plug."

Dear Reader,

For Joseph Brentjens's story, "The End of the Plug," which is fast-paced and action-packed, we decided to focus on making the ending more satisfying. Joseph and I agreed that an author can have the best opening in the world, but, if his or her ending is flat, then readers are left feeling unfulfilled.

When we discussed satisfying endings, we talked about endings that meet readers' expectations and needs. When stories are about characters in conflict, readers want to see that conflict resolved by those characters. Supporting characters can help the story's main character, but, in order for a book's ending to be satisfying, the protagonist has to solve his or her own problems.

Imagine if Dumbledore had suddenly shown up at the end of the Harry Potter series to battle Voldemort? That would have left readers feeling cheated. Voldemort is Harry's problem, and readers want to see Harry deal with Voldemort himself.

Authors also want to be sure that their main characters resolve their conflicts with the tools they're given earlier in the story. Readers need to have the seeds of resolution planted throughout the story so that its ending is fulfilling. For instance, if your hero has been fighting a dragon for a hundred pages, the protagonist can't just suddenly remember—on page 98—that he has

a magic sword in his closet.

After you've finished writing your story, go back and make sure that you've established your main character's problem and that your main character is the one who resolves it, using the tools you've given him or her. Because the conclusion is your last chance to speak to your readers, make sure it leaves them feeling rewarded for reading your story.

Happy Writing,

J.J. Austrian is working on his epic scientific fantasy, *The Silver Coffin*, while trying not to drive his family crazy by pretending to be the captain of the *U.S.S. Enterprise* and screaming "Kahn!" at the dinner table. He has an MFA in Writing for Children and Young Adults from Hamline University and lives in Minneapolis, Minnesota.

Joseph Brentjens

Joseph is a seventh-grade boy at Chowan Middle School in Edenton, North Carolina. He loves to read, write, and play games on the computer. He wants to become an accomplished author later in his life.

Here are some of Joseph's thoughts on the writing and revision of "The End of the Plug."

What's your favorite part about writing?

Probably the idea process. Coming up with a world where you control what happens. For once, after reading all the books where you thought they should have done this or that, you get to choose.

Your story has a very interesting antagonist. How did you come up with that idea?

From all the times my parents were telling me to get off the computer and talking about electricity and electronics like they're a villain.

What is your writing process?

I usually write down the idea on a piece of paper but prefer to write the story on the computer, since my handwriting is the worst you'll ever find.

How did changing your ending work for you?

I decided to add a whole different element to the story, so now there is a new object that's introduced early in the story and helps tie together the ending.

If you had to take one book with you to a desert island what would it be?

One book? That I would never get bored with? *Heroes of Olympus,* by Rick Riordan, which is really a series, or *Ungifted* by Gordam Koran.

Luke Skywalker vs Harry Potter. Who wins?

Well, I'd have to say Luke Skywalker. Take away the light saber and wand, Harry basically has nothing, but Luke still has the force.*

***It was a trick question. The correct answer is: Gandalf**

278

The End of the Plug

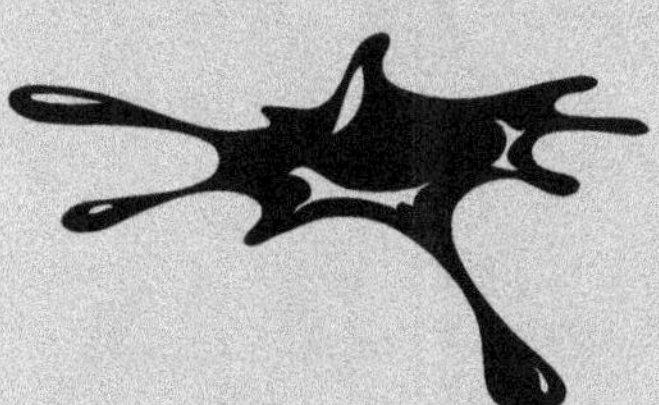

by Joseph Brentjens

280

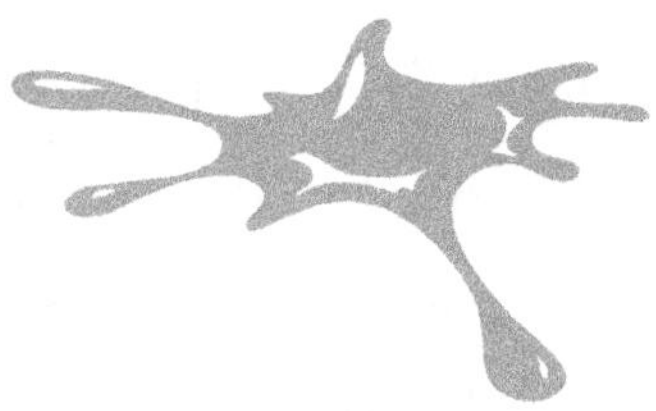

May 16th, 2020

They called him Simon. Simon was no different from you or me. He went to school, he had no powers, had to do essays, which he hated like almost every kid (although he was interested by this essay about an invention called the heat rocket), just your overall average kid. Black hair, glasses, lives with his parents; if you saw him you would have thought nothing of him. However, he was a computer whiz. If he ran into a problem on the computer, he could usually solve it in a matter of seconds. In eighth grade, he was even voted most likely to become the next Steve Jobs!

By tenth grade, he had not changed a bit. One day, though, there was a computer problem that confused Simon. Error 27764. Simon had never heard of such a thing. He thought it was a practical joke played on him by one of his friends, but soon, after multiple warnings, he realized that it would take a technical genius to create such a virus, and none of his friends were technical geniuses. For once, Simon was clueless about a computer error.

He called Tech Support. They checked his computer and did every method of fixing they knew, but the warnings kept popping up. However, they did figure out that it did no real damage to the computer itself. He was bewildered. A computer virus that didn't do any damage to the software? He refused to believe it. His search for answers was fruitless. He spent days and days by the computer, shaking it and screaming. It was driving him mad, he knew, but he just couldn't stop trying. He had never had this trouble before and it made him angry and confused.

Finally, one day he found on an online social media site that someone named Phil (a computer whiz like Simon) had the same error. Phil went mad trying to fix it, and even got suspended because of the days he chose to work on the computer instead of going to school. He went missing after a few weeks of madness. There was no trace of him anywhere. It was almost like he disappeared into thin air. The only thing they found out of place from the last minute he was seen was the plug of the computer was out.

This gave Simon an idea. What if he pulled the plug on his computer like Phil did? He was about to do it when he had another thought. What if the plug is why he is missing? He thought about it for a second but then didn't consider the question anymore because he thought it was impossible. Simon then went up to the computer and pulled all the cords out at once. That was the last thing he saw.

"Welcome, Simon. Took you long enough."

Simon woke from a deep sleep to those words. Simon lifted his head and looked around. He was surrounded by darkness with the occasional flash of lightning. He had no idea where he was or how he got there. He was all alone and confused. As if that wasn't scary enough, he was standing on nothing.

"Why so shy? Don't act like you don't know me."

Simon had no idea where the voice was coming from. It seemed to just appear from the darkness.

"I'm sorry, but I don't know you," Simon said, sounding scared for the first time in his life.

"Oh Simon, can't you tell who I am? Look around you. Think of the last thing you did. Is it really that complicated for such a great mind like yours?"

The last thing he did was pull the plugs. He put two and two together.

"You must be my computer," Simon said with confidence.

The voice sighed. "That is a good guess, but I'm afraid that you are a little off. I make computers work. I am the biggest part of everyone's lives. I am what people need to survive today. I am Electricity. I am what the earth revolves around!"

Simon stopped moving. He was talking to Electricity. He could hardly comprehend it all.

"Well then, Electricity, why am I here?" Electricity stopped for a second, as if it was buffering.

"Well, Simon. There is an issue. You humans abuse my power. You use me for the dumbest things. Cheating on tests, looking up pictures of your neighbor's cat, THE DUMBEST THINGS! As a result of all your stupidity, I have decided to turn everything against you. All of your beloved devices will come alive and take over with me as the sole ruler of the world."

"If that's your plan, then what do I have to do with that?"

"You see, Simon, I'm gathering the people that know more about me than me! People like you fall for my trick. In order to get you here, I need a direct connection with you, like being struck by lightning. That was taking too long and I didn't have time for it, so I lured people like you with a virus that can only be destroyed by pulling the computer's plug. In everyone's madness to find a cure, you all forget all about the safety procedures and pulled the plug too quickly, you get shocked, I bring you here. Easy as fixing Error 404."

"Where are we, anyway?" Simon asked.

"Outside of the universe. The dwelling of Electricity. There is no time here. I am the only one that can control what time you are in when you go back in the universe."

"You weren't kidding when you said the universe revolves around you."

"Obviously not. Since when does Electricity lie?" Simon could barely hold in the laugh. "Yes, I am well aware of the pop-up ads and viruses and such but that was never me. That was humanity. I was a great thing 'til used incorrectly. You have no one to blame but yourselves." Simon looked downward with a feeling of guilt. He had created plenty of fake ads and viruses in his day to get back at his friends.

"Now that you have no more questions I guess that we will be going now."

"Going where?"

"Here."

Simon heard a crackle. Then darkness.

Simon awoke in an actual solid room. The room was completely empty. No windows, no decorations, nothing. At least this time though he could feel the ground.

"This is an empty room. You can decorate it however you wish."

"How am I supposed to do that?"

"Ever heard of imagination? Now, hurry up. You're going to be late to your new job."

Job? Simon didn't like the sound of that. "What new job? What do you mean?"

There was no answer, for Electricity had left. Simon had no way to get out. He was stuck.

"Well, if I'm going to be here awhile, I might as well take a shot at decorating this place," he said to himself.

Now all he had to do was to figure out how. He thought about how Electricity said *imagination*. He did the only thing he could think of. Imagine the stuff.

He pointed his finger to a corner and said, "I want a computer there."

In an instant it appeared. He went on the computer. "Ahh, the one thing that even exists outside the universe, Wi-Fi."

Right then he got what he thought was the best idea ever. He tried to go on Facebook. He could send someone a message to help him escape! When he tried, it redirected him to a website that said at the top, "SHAME ON YOU." Then he felt a big shock on his arm. The shock forced him to the ground.

He lifted his sleeve. He saw a reddish tally mark burned on to his arm. Electricity is too clever, he thought. He had one last idea, though.

Electricity can only control electronics. What if he made a door?

He pointed a finger at a wall. "I want a door there."

He felt no shock, but he saw a door. It worked. Simon was frightened to open the door, but he knew it was the only way to escape. He opened the door.

He came into a new room like his. A boy about Simon's age was on the other side if the room. His back was turned and he didn't see or hear him. Simon snuck up behind him put his hand over the boy's mouth. The boy uttered a muffled scream. After Simon calmed him down he let the guy talk.

"Who are you?" the guy asked. "Did Electricity send you to kill me? I'm working as hard as I can!"

"It's okay. I'm trying to escape. My name is Simon. I came from that door I made with my mind. Who are you?"

"Phil," he said. Simon had to stop for a second. It was the guy from the social media site!

"Phil? Everyone says you're missing!"

"Like anyone cares…"

"Your parents do. A lot. Listen, we don't exactly have time for talking. We have to escape. Are you with me or not?" Phil looked up at Simon and gave him a nod.

"So what can we imagine that could get us out of here?" Simon asked him.

Phil finally stood up. He never turned down a chance to be strategic. "What if we imagine a molecule capturer?"

"What's that?" Simon Asked.

"It's like a bottle that captures molecules, it keeps them

alive but contains them, but it needs to be taken from a solid object, not a gas. So keep on thinking!"

Simon thought for another second then yelled, "Wait! I got it! Electricity runs most forms of transportation today, but what about other forms?"

"I get it! Like manual power!" exclaimed Phil, now understanding Simon's excitement.

"EXACTLY!" Simon said with a laugh. "Now you're getting it! We need to make something that runs on us! That WE control! Not that blasted Electricity!"

"What would that be? "

"The heat rocket."

The heat rocket is an invention made a few months before Simon came to this land. Its purpose was to be more eco-friendly. It runs completely on body heat generated by pedaling.

"ARE YOU NUTS? We can't work that thing, much less steer it!" protested Phil.

"We need that to escape. It's our only option. We are still outside the universe and need something with enough power to escape this place!"

"Fine," Phil said regretfully. Phil extended his pointer finger to the side of the room. "I want a heat rocket." They both saw the room grow larger in size. As soon as the room settled down, it only took a second for the rocket to stare them in the face.

They both got inside the rocket. "How will we know that we will arrive at our time?" Phil thought out loud.

Simon paused for a few seconds. He was right.

"It doesn't matter. This is our chance to escape and we have to take it." They both sat on the chair. The chair had bicycle pedals at the end for exercising. They needed to exercise to get it working. They both got ready and started pedaling. They could hear they biggest invention of the millennium power up and lift off. They heard the sound of the roof smashing. Five seconds later there was another crash and then another. Finally there was silence. "I think we have made it." Phil said with relief. He spoke too soon. They heard a loud crash and a screech that would put a lion's roar to shame.

"YOU DARE LEAVE MY DOMAIN? YOU BELONG HERE!" screamed the familiar voice of Electricity. "Pedal faster, Phil!" Simon shouted. They tried to get as much heat as they could, yet it was no use. Electricity had found them.

"I may not be able to control the ship but I can still control lightning!" The two boys heard a crackle. Electricity shot their ship.

"Phil, we need to get to the escape pods now!" They busted out of the cockpit and ran for the escape pod. They reached the escape hatch at about the same time that they started losing altitude.

However, there was a problem. There was only one pod that could only carry one person.

"Phil, you go."

"No! You tried to save me. You deserve it." Crackle. Electricity was almost there.

"Phil," Simon said, "I'm not going to stay here arguing. You need to go now. You will only make it if you go NOW!"

Simon shoved him in and yelled, "Now start pedaling!" Simon saw his feet go and the pod leave. He heard the final crackle. The last thing he saw before passing out for the third time was the pod disappear. Phil had made it.

Simon woke up for what he hoped was the last time that day. He felt a sting on his arm again. He now saw four tally marks on his skin.

"That was some plan you tried to pull back there. Too bad you didn't make it. Now get back to work!!! Your job is to create viruses. You make them the way you would a computer one but it will be a virus that will infect and kill people. You have five days to make a prototype."

"Wait! Is Phil safe?" There was no response. It may have said nothing, but Electricity's silence said it all. His friend was safe. He couldn't believe that his skills were being used against his own race. He still had to try and create one, though, or else he would die. He sat down at his computer. Just a prototype in five days. Couldn't be that hard. He moved his mouse over to the new icon on his screen, which he could tell was the right icon because of its name: Virus Creator Deluxe. He clicked it. It had a simple format that was similar to all the others, but this one had a section that said: *Test your virus*. He didn't click on it yet. He had to make a virus first. He started working.

Four and a half days passed and he still couldn't find a good virus. He was used to making viruses for computers. Not for humans. This thought gave him an idea. He had twelve hours to make his idea reality. He had to work fast.

Simon looked at his clock. It had been five days.

"Simon! Have you made a successful prototype?" Asked an eager Electricity.

"Even better! I made a complete one. I have put the complete formula in this bottle."

Simon picked up the bottle that was sitting on the desk. "Take a look."

Simon felt an invisible force pull the bottle out of his hand.

"The formula intoxicates any human who smells it. They then only have a week to live. It shouldn't be toxic to anything else, though." He hoped that Electricity was just as curious as humans.

He was correct. He saw the force open the bottle. Electricity roared with pain.

"Oops, I forgot. I left the human formula on my bed!" said Simon.

"Then what is this?!" demanded Electricity.

"It's the same thing," Simon replied. "Only this one intoxicates everything that ISN'T humans! Oops!"

Electricity roared again. "You have made your final mistake, Simon! Enjoy the electric prison!"

Simon felt the sting, which he recognized as the final tally. He, for the fourth time, heard the sound of lighting and blacked out.

Solid brick. The first thing Simon saw. He was in a prison. No one else was there, though.

"Welcome to the Electric prison. You are the first one here. The first one to disobey me." Electricity coughed. "Your virus has taken a toll on me, Simon. I do not appreciate that. While I only have a week to live, I will devote that whole week to making sure that you are tortured to the point that you have no words left to say but 'help,' and in my final breath I will make sure that you and everyone in my domain dies with me."

Despite Simon's fear, he knew he had to stay cocky and confident.

"Sounds fun!"

This enraged Electricity more than ever. "Is this fun?"

Electricity shot a bolt of lightning at him. "No? What about this?" Simon got shot again. He was knocked down but not unconscious.

"Is that all you got?" asked Simon.

"I'm just beginning, friend!" He shot him more and more.

No matter how many volts filled him, Simon still wouldn't pass out or die. Simon had to end this. He saw only one way. Before electricity could hit him again, Simon ran full speed to it. From the knowledge he got from school he knew what would happen. Lighting (or Electricity in this case) strikes the highest object around, and in this room, that was him. He absorbed Electricity and fell in the ground in pain. Simon was part electricity now; therefore, the poison partially harmed him. He was about to pass out again, he knew, but before he did he saw a man in a suit that appeared out of nowhere pick him up.

May 16th, 2080

Simon woke in a bed. He felt a sting on his foot. He looked and saw the man putting a needle in his foot. The needle was connected to a bottle.

Simon sat up and said, "Where am I? Who are you?" Simon asked.

The man sighed. "You're in a hospital on Earth, and don't you recognize me?"

Simon studied his looks. "I'm sorry, I can't say that I do."

The man sighed once again. "It's me, Simon. Phil."

Simon couldn't help but gasp. "Phil? What happened?"

"Well it's a long story. After I left the place I panicked. I almost went crazy from it. Lucky for me it was the year 2040 and they had enough technology to sense a heat rocket from light years away. They teleported me back to earth. They said that I just suddenly appeared on their screens. They sent me back to my normal life, but my parents had already passed. So I was sent to an orphanage. That was when I met Suzie. Suzie and I both never got adopted and finally, after both of us went to college, we got married. We had children and I got a job as a scientist and inventor. I one day realized that I could actually track down the end of the universe if I could just get the escape pod. The escape pod, a few years after I came back, crash landed on earth. I was able to contact people to get it. I performed my tests and got a loan to hire people geared with the latest inventions to willingly come with me to go to the end of the universe. So we traveled there, waited for the correct time, went in at the correct time, and found you and everyone else. Electricity is now contained in this molecule capturer."

Simon looked at the dark smoke that filled the bottle before him. It took a while to soak it in.

"How were you years older when you had just left?" Simon asked.

"Remember? He controls what time the outside world is. We just had good timing."

Simon remembered now. "What am I supposed to do now?"

"Go back to life, I guess."

"My parents are dead too, though. Aren't they?"

Phil put his hand on his shoulder. "I'm sorry."

"I don't know what to do." Simon said, on the verge of tears. "They were all I had."

Phil removed his hand from Simon's shoulder. "You can

do what I did—go to an orphanage until you can get a job and support yourself."

Simon felt a tad bit of worry of what would become of him.

"At least one good thing came out of this," Phil said after a moment of silence. "Now we can use Electricity's powers without him watching us."

"Yeah, I guess we can."

Playing with Line Breaks

Sarah Lyn Rogers mentored Alister Sharp through a revision focused on playing with line breaks in Alister's poem, "Jamaican Lake."

Dear Reader,

When I read the first draft of Alister Sharp's poem about a family trip to Jamaica, I was struck by her usage of sensory details and the way that she built structure into the poem using different forms of repetition. Repeating the words at the beginning of a line ("into the lake, into the cold") is a poetic device called anaphora, used by famous poets like Walt Whitman! Alister has great instincts as a young poet.

The main opportunity I found for revision in this poem was the chance to play with line breaks. In Alister's first draft, the poem was written like prose, the kind of writing I am using right now, where the words on the page get cut off only because they reach the margin. This type of writing is used for fiction, nonfiction essays, and pretty much everything that isn't poetry, because the focus in prose is on what is being said.

Poetry offers the power to control how the words are said, which is where line breaks come in. The end of a line determines which word has the most impact. For Alister's poem, I encouraged her to add line breaks to emphasize words that were important to her, and to discover and highlight hidden patterns in her work. I advised Alister to try a few different versions of line breaks in her poem. None of her original words were changed, to show how changing only the form of a poem can make it very different!

In your own poetry, try breaking the lines in new places, and then break them again. You can find gems hidden in your writing if you mine for them.

Happy revising!

Sarah

Sarah Lyn Rogers is this year's winner of the Academy of American Poets - Virginia de Araujo prize. Her essays, poetry, and stories have been published in *3Elements Review, Vine Leaves Literary Journal,* and *Reed Magazine,* among others. When she isn't writing or working with Young Inklings, Sarah is an assistant fiction editor for *The Rumpus.*

Alister Sharp

Alister is a ten-year-old girl in Los Altos Hills, CA. She enjoys traveling with her family, meeting new people, reading and going to amusement parks. Alister recently was a finalist in an Eber & Wein poetry contest. She takes dance three days a week and loves it. Now if you'll excuse her, she's off to read.

Here are some of Alister's thoughts on the writing and revision of "Jamaican Lake."

Your revision goal was to play with line breaks. How did it feel to rearrange your poem this way?

It was pretty fun. I like mixing around the words and trying to see what worked.

Did you try it a few different ways? How did you decide when the line breaks felt right?

I just kind of knew. I tried a couple other ways but I didn't like them.

Did you notice more patterns in your poem when you were playing with different line breaks? How did patterns jump out at you?

Some I knew, some popped out, like some rhymes. Those were fun to play around with.

What was your favorite part of the *Inklings Book* process?

I liked working on it and putting in the line breaks.

Do you have a favorite place where you like to write?

Not really. When we move, I'm probably going to write on my beanbag pile.

What are you working on now?

I'm writing a story about people with superhuman powers like freezing time, turning invisible, and reading people's minds. They got stuck in a parallel universe and they have to get out.

What advice do you have for other young poets?

Put out what's in your mind even if you don't think it's going to work, because it might turn out to be a really great line!

Jamaican Lake

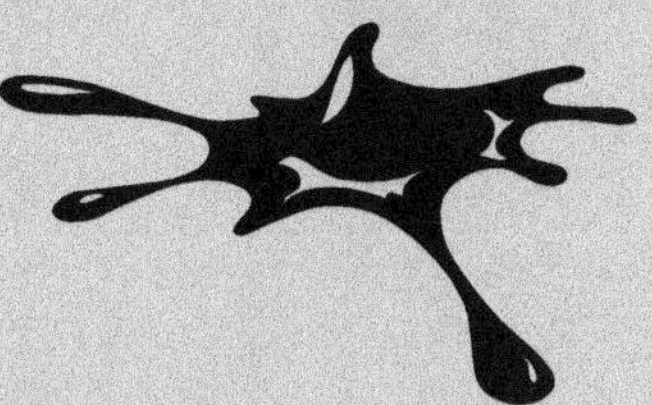

by

Alister Sharp

302

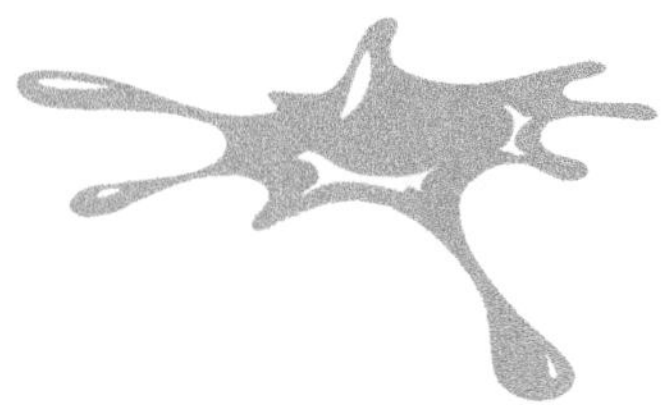

As the ocean laps my toes.

Jamaican air blows bringing

the smell of pineapple

the sound of laughter

the feeling of happiness

the sensation of friends

Up into the woods.

Onto the rope, and swish

Back, and suddenly I'm flying.

Into the lake

into the cold

Jamaican Lake

into family.

Plunge.

Underwater.

green swirls around me.

I'm wanted

I'm where I'm supposed to be.

And that's all that matters

Playing with Rhythm

Naomi Kinsman mentored Naomi Fuller through a revision focused on playing with rhythm in Naomi's poem, "Thunder Booms."

Dear Reader,

One of the very first things that stood out to me about Naomi's poem was the way it begged to be read out loud. While not every poem has a distinct rhythm or even needs one, "Thunder Booms" was clearly structured for sound. The rhythm literally danced off the page. I read it out loud a few times and then said, "This is going to be FUN!"

In our revision, Naomi and I focused on rhythm, working to make what was already strong even stronger. "Thunder Booms" already had a strong beat on which we were able to build. To start, we read each line aloud together and noticed where we felt the rhythm worked perfectly. Then, we looked for places where a different word might make the lines read even more smoothly.

When we found words that didn't quite fit, there was the inevitable moment of worry. Sometimes it is hard to think of any other word when we've found one that we want to use. When we hit those snags, we tried a few strategies. First, we brainstormed. In a couple cases, Naomi looked up some words in her rhyming dictionary or a thesaurus. Sometimes making the rhythm work meant changing a couple words in a line.

One important note. We noticed that sometimes breaking the rhythmic pattern was the just-right thing to do. When we broke the rhythm, we were able to call attention to words and phrases. Since we set up the

strong rhythm throughout, even tiny breaks in the overall beat caused pauses and emphasis.

In the end, we found that the best way to play with the rhythm was to use our ears and to read the poem over and over.

Naomi didn't end up changing many words at all in her poem, but the ones she changed made a huge overall impact on the flow of her poem. We encourage you: whether you write poetry OR prose, read it aloud! We're sure you'll make interesting discoveries.

Happy Writing,

Naomi

Naomi Kinsman is the author of *Spilled Ink, A Young Writer's Notebook*, and the *From Sadie's Sketchbook* series. One of her favorite parts about having founded Society of Young Inklings is meeting and working with so many talented young authors. She has an MFA in Writing for Children and Young Adults from Hamline University and lives in San Jose, CA.

Naomi Fuller

Naomi is a second grader at Shoal Creek Elementary. She loves art—especially painting still life—and writing personal narratives. Her favorite swim stroke is the breast stroke, and she likes to play sports with her twin brother. She loves Oreo cookies!

Here are some of Naomi's thoughts on the writing and revision of "Thunder Booms."

What inspired "Thunder Booms?"

Well, I like to write about storms because they are scary.

How did it feel to revise your poem?

It felt kind of good and kind of not. It was hard because all of my hard work was being revised. It was good to have something new because my revision is different than the first one. Revising is good because you can have a different version of your work and add more detail.

Did you like this poem better after it was revised?

I like it better because it has more of a rhythm.

You didn't change very many words because your poem already had a strong rhythm. How did you choose which words to change?

I read the poem out loud and some parts didn't sound right. Then, I would brainstorm and let myself think for a couple days and then come back to the parts I wanted to change. My mom helped me a little. One way she helped was that she came up with a word and then I came up with a word and we tried to make the words fit into the syllables we needed.

What advice would you give other writers about writing and revising poetry?

Well, revising is hard because sometimes it's hard to think of new ideas, because you really have your heart set on a certain word or phrase. But sometimes you can use resources to try to make the poem better, such as a rhyming dictionary or a friend or family member.

Do you have a place you like to write?

Sometimes in my room or at school, or even sitting on the couch. The space can be loud or quiet, it doesn't matter to me.

Are you working on any new writing?

At school, I'm writing a how-to article, where you have to tell the reader how to do something. I'm giving directions on how to make a craft called Crazy Caterpillars.

Do you ever feel stuck in your writing?

Sometimes I feel stuck and so I wait a day or two and try to think about something else and then I come back to it. A lot of times I'm out somewhere and an idea just pops into my head.

How do you get your ideas?

A lot of my ideas are like personal narrative because I like to write about things that actually happened to me.

Thunder Booms

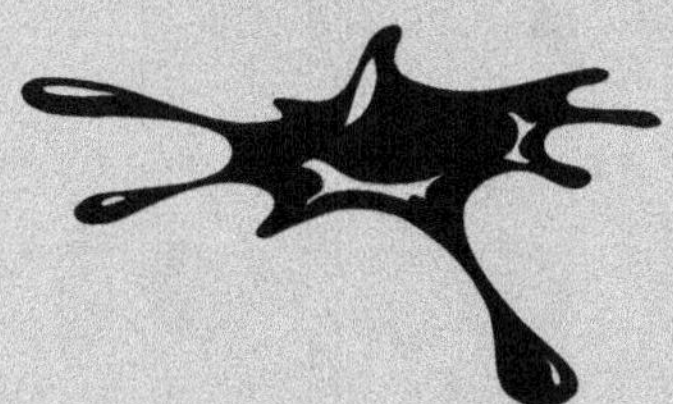

by
Naomi Fuller

312

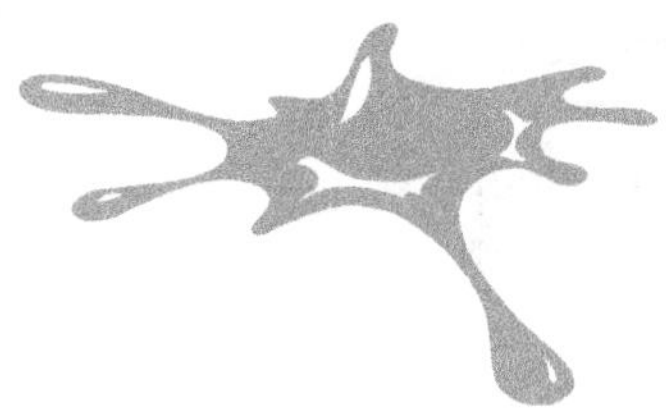

My yard is looking cracked and dry.

A bolt of lightning fills the sky!

Thunder BOOMS!

It shakes my room!

I shiver, scared.

I hug my bear.

CRACK!

The clock goes blank.

Is this a prank?

Thunder Booms

I grab my blankets, filled with fright.

The wind is howling through the night.

I lie there in a trembling heap,

And somehow I fall fast asleep.

HONK!

Was that a car?

How bizarre!

A sound of peace, oh so sweet —

The birds are singing, "Tweet! Tweet! Tweet!"

I slept right through the storm, I bet.

And now my yard looks soft and wet.

Line Structure

Mandy Davis mentored Carmen Bechtel through a revision focused on line structure in Carmen's poem, "Earth."

Dear Reader,

Structure is basically how something is put together. If we are looking at a whole poem, structure is the order of the lines. Line structure is how the words are put together in each line of text. In poetry, where your words go is just as important as what your words are.

Carmen Bechtel's poem, "Earth," included so many visual images we wanted to make sure that these images took center stage. So, in her revision, she worked on highlighting these images through their placement in each line of her poem. Here is an example of one of the changes she made in line structure.

Original: I watch seasons change like a seed sprouts into a flower.

Revised: My seasons change like a seedling sprouts into a flower.

In the original line, the words "I watch" create a filter. It's as if we are seeing the seasons changing through someone else's eyes. Take those words away, and we're seeing the seasons change right in front of our own eyes. We don't have to read through unnecessary words to get to the image. The image is right there at the beginning of the line.

Look at the lines of your own poem. Underline the images, the things you can see. Try putting your images at the beginning of some of your lines. Does it change the feel of your poem? Remove bits of text that you

think you might not need. See how your poem changes. Remember: don't be afraid to take words out. You can always add them back in later if you feel like you need them.

Poems are as different as people. Not all poems need imagery at the beginning of each line. Maybe in your poem the most important images are at the end of each line. That would be a different kind of line structure. The most important thing to remember when revising a poem is that where you put each word really does matter!

Happy Revising!

Mandy

Mandy Davis is the author of the forthcoming middle grade novel *Stuperstar*. She has an MFA in Writing for Children and Young Adults from Hamline University and has taught writing at the elementary and middle school levels for six years. She lives and writes in Minneapolis, Minnesota.

Carmen Bechtel

Carmen is in fourth grade at Corte Madera School. She enjoys biking on the San Francisco Bay Trail with her family, jumping on her trampoline, and swinging on her rope swing. She loves animals, especially her two cats, Jacko and Stoker. One of Carmen's hobbies is filmmaking. She works mainly in the comedy-horror genre. Carmen also dabbles in stop-motion animation.

Here are some of Carmen's thoughts on the writing and revision of "Earth."

How did changing line structure change your poem?

> Words are not as powerful if they don't make you see a picture in your mind. So, I worked on each line and focused on trying to make each line into a picture. I did this by changing where the words were placed in each line (line structure) and taking out some of the words that I didn't need anymore. Now when people read each line, they immediately see a picture in their minds.

On your original draft, the last line of your poem was: "My name is Mother Earth and this is my poem." Why did you decide to take that line out of your revised draft?

The words "My name is Mother Earth and this is my poem" don't paint a picture. They don't really mean anything. So, I took them out and let my final line be: "I stand here, grass beneath my toes and my hands in the air." This line is a repeat of the first line in my poem. I like beginning and ending with the picture of Mother Earth.

How did you come up with the line: "I have a heart made of rubies that erupts out of mountains"?

I wrote this line just after we learned about volcanoes in school. When you draw a heart, you usually make them red—the same color as lava. So I brainstormed all the different reddish colors and came up with rubies. Also in this line, I was comparing the earth to us. The center of the earth is made of magma and the center of us is made of our hearts.

Where did you get the idea of writing a poem from the Earth's perspective?

I really love nature and wanted to write a poem that represented nature. Also, lots of people call the earth, Mother Earth, so that gave me the idea of writing the poem from the Earth's perspective, like the Earth is actually a person. I wanted to create something that would represent Earth's beauty and give people another way to appreciate the Earth.

Why do you like writing poems?

When you write a story, it takes longer to describe everything. Poems let you get your thoughts out in a deeper way with fewer words. In a story, you have to fill in all the different parts. Poems are an easier way to express feelings.

Earth

by
Carmen Bechtel

322

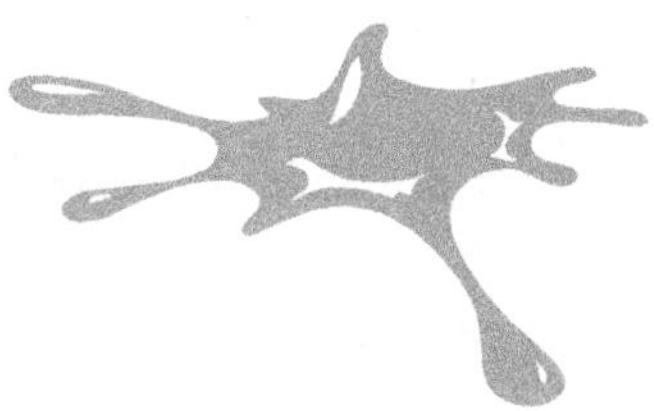

I stand here, grass beneath my toes and my hands in the air.

My hair is golden sunshine and a snowflake scarf wraps around me.

I watch over deer trotting through my velvet blue streams.

Birds soar through my sparkling breezes or through my starry night skies.

My seasons change like a seedling sprouts into a flower.

When I fall asleep, the moon and owls come to say good night.

When I awaken, a golden, pink, and purple beam lightly sails into the sky, saying good morning.

I let out a thousand silver tears when I cry that land on everyone below me.

My squishy white bed floats through the sky.

I have a heart made of rubies that erupts out of mountains.

I stand here, grass beneath my toes and my hands in the air.

Prose into Poetry

Naomi Kinsman mentored Cameron Shaw through a revision focused on simplifying prose into poetry in Cameron's poem, "Camper Meant for Two: A Grandparent Memory."

Dear Reader,

One of my favorite things about Cameron's poem was the way she used simple, strong words in the poem to create a rich picture. Some of my favorite words included "piled," "greasy" and "lollipops." When I read those words, I felt as though I was crammed in with her in the camper van, melting in the heat on the riverbank and then splashing in the river.

Also, Cameron zoomed in on the moments from her trip

that were the most meaningful. Along with carefully choosing each word, poets also zoom in on small moments. They highlight everything that is important and cut all the rest away. Poets make every word count.

In our revision, we focused on making pictures in a reader's mind. We looked for all the strong words in the poem and made them stand out by cutting out all the extra words. We also found words that weren't working as hard for Cameron as they could, and brainstormed new ones that would bring the experience to life with vivid detail and emotion.

Here's the process that we used:

1. First, we read one stanza.
2. On a separate piece of paper, we wrote a list of words that fit with this moment: thinking about verbs, nouns, and adjectives.
3. Then, we underlined a few words on the list that we wanted to add to the poem.
4. Next, we reworked the stanza, adding line breaks, new words and cutting out any words we didn't need.
5. Finally, we re-read the stanza and pictured the

moment. We asked ourselves: will the reader be able to picture it too? Is there anything else to add or take away?

Using this process, we were able to cut away what was extra and highlight the most important parts of this poem. If you have a highly descriptive story, consider trying this process and transforming your story into a poem. Why? When we play with form, we are able to see our writing with fresh eyes. This new perspective can't help but add layers and new dimensions to our writing.

In Creativity,

Naomi

Naomi Kinsman is the author of *Spilled Ink, A Young Writer's Notebook*, and the *From Sadie's Sketchbook* series. One of her favorite parts about having founded Society of Young Inklings is meeting and working with so many talented young authors. She has an MFA in Writing for Children and Young Adults from Hamline University and lives in San Jose, CA.

Cameron Shaw

Cameron was born in California but moved to North Carolina when she was nine years old. She is currently in fifth grade at Elkin Elementary. She is usually busy with school, but when she has free time she enjoys reading, writing, crafting, playing with her sister and two brothers, and so much more. When she grows up, Cameron hopes to be a lawyer, an actress, and an author.

Here are some of Cameron's thoughts on the writing and revision of "A Camper Meant for Two: A Grandparent Memory."

How did you feel about the revision process?

It was hard and kind of fun. There were all sorts of ways I could change things, so I had to decide which one I was going to do. Deciding was hard.

How did you decide where to put line breaks?

I put them where they sounded right and also to separate different ideas.

We worked on turning what read more like a story into a poem during the revision. What advice do you have for other poets about how to do the same thing?

> I'd tell them to read the story and change the words to make it into a poem. Try to describe things more clearly in the poem. In a story, you describe what happens but in a poem you describe what you see and feel.

Did you change more or less than you expected to change?

> I changed a little less than I expected to have to change. I thought we might have to do more during our second meeting, but I think we changed just the right amount. If I'd done less, I wouldn't feel like I'd worked hard, but it I'd done more it would have been overwhelming.

How did you find the words that felt just right?

> I went through and marked what I wanted to change. If I didn't know what to do right away, then I'd go on to the next section. When I went on, it was easier to think of a word for the question I'd left behind.

How do you get ideas?

> Some of them come from real life experiences, and some come from what you wish would happen. Some just show up.

Where do you like to write?

At the kitchen table because we do everything there—eat, do homework, make crafts—so it's sort of a central place and it's comfortable too because I'm there a lot. It's also relaxing because everyone is usually in another room and I feel like I belong and it's my place. And I also like to write on my bed because it's comfortable.

What is your favorite kind of writing?

My favorite thing to write is fantasy. But that's one of the hardest things to write because you have to invent everything. Getting started is the hardest part.

Do you have advice for other young writers?

Come up with a plan and if you can't think of what word you want to put somewhere leave a space and come back. And if you can't think of anything, talk to someone like a friend or family member.

Sometimes if I don't finish a story, I put it in a binder. Then if I can't think of a new story, I go through the binder and choose one of my older ideas.

A Camper Meant for Two: A Grandparent Memory

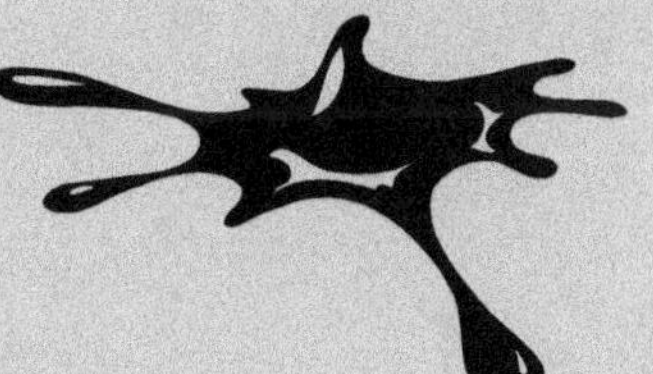

by

Cameron Shaw

332

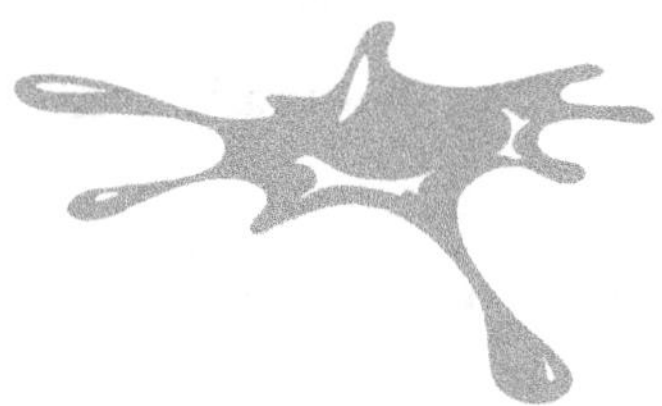

We all piled into the camper van.

The three of us, with enough smiles and hugs to go around the world 100 times.

We were so excited. Three whole days at the river! What more could we wish for?

We snuggled into the mud green seats.
It was a long ride, but we weren't bored. We were together, in a small camper meant for two.

We saw camper vans through the trees and knew we were almost there.

Then we smelled smoke.

We pulled in the parking lot and men began spraying the camper van
with water.

It took forever, but we finally went to the river.

I remember

the greasy sunscreen, the hot sun, and the cool water.

I remember.

We started with our toes, and eventually, we just jumped.

The water felt refreshing.

We swam, we floated, we walked, we jumped.

We tried to catch fish with a net. That didn't work too well.

We sat,

and sat,

and sat.

We didn't catch anything, but someone gave us fish

and we kept them until we had to let them go.

We saw two snakes. They scared me half to death.

Remember?

And you said we wouldn't see any!

We rode tubes in the rapids, and one time, we got free ice cream. That
was exciting!

Sometimes, I would ride on your bike or play at the park.

I always wondered why there was a park near the river, but it didn't
matter.

It was fun anyway.

I liked your bike.

It was old fashioned and a little rusty, but it was fast!

Remember when you thought the lollibands were lollipops?

Silly you, they were hair bands.

We got one for Leah.

At night, I slept on the sofa bed in that camper meant for two.

I helped make dinner, did Sudoku and watched a movie.

Going to the river was one of my favorite trips

I'll always cherish the special times we've had together.

But, then we all piled into the camper van and headed home.

The three of us, with enough smiles and hugs to go around the world

100 times.

Playing with Tone

Polly McCann mentored Sophia Calegari through a revision focused on playing with tone in Sophia's poem, "Secret Star."

Dear Reader,

Sophia's poem, "Secret Star," is a beautiful, well-crafted poem in first-person narration. We chose to focus our revision on tone. When talking about poetry, we usually call the voice in the poem "the speaker." Why? A poem may be written from any point of view, not only the poet's viewpoint. A poem could be in the voice of a historical person, an inanimate object, or an imaginary character. The tone emerges from the emotions, style and intention of that voice.

In her revision, I directed Sophia to really focus on her

verbs in order to strengthen the voice in her poem. Poems are lyrical. The words are few and chosen for meaning as well as sound. So Sophia considered each of these aspects of each verb. You can do the same revision to your writing by asking these two questions:

In your poem, does each action verb do what you want it to do?

Sophia's poem had great verbs: showering, wandering, walk, light, reflect, seek. I asked her to look at the verbs ending with "ing." This ending means they are continuing to take place. Sophia tried them without the "ing" to see if they were stronger. It made a lot more sense for the speaker in her poem to tell the star to "wander" than to describe it as "wandering." Sophia really emphasized that the speaker had a message for the star person in this poem, not simply the desire to describe one.

Where is the heart message of your poem, or the central line? When you think about the key verb in this line, what associations or feelings do you have about that word?

Sophia had a great central line in her poem. We both tried several different verbs or similes to replace the word verb, "are." Like trying on different shoes, each

one gave a different message.

"For your secrets/ Are with me"
Your dark secrets/ Stay safe with me
Your bright secrets/ Belong to us alone
Your quiet secrets/ I'll never know
Your secrets,/ Like a black hole
Let go of your secrets/ Hold them out to the night
Let go of your dark/ Reveal your light

Fun isn't it? Each new verb or simile changed the tone or the flavor of the whole poem. You, the writer, direct the tone with your speaker's voice—and great verbs help too.

Keep Writing,

Polly

Polly McCann, artist and writer, received her MFA in writing from Hamline University. She studied poetry under Julia Kasdorf and workshopped with Ron Koertge. Currently she is working on several biographies, novels, and books of poetry. *Tea with Alice* is the title for her collection of autobiographical poems; three generations of stories retold in free verse. You can find her under a rainbow in Kansas City with her two children and their dog, Spencer.

Sophia Calegari

Sophia is in the fifth grade at Wade Thomas Elementary School, in Marin County. She enjoys athletic sports, such as soccer, and does ballet at Stapleton School of the Performing Arts. She loves writing poetry and stories because they take her to another world, where she can express her feelings in words, full of anything she can imagine. Sophia also enjoys reading, especially dystopian novels. When she grows up, she wants to become an author, so she can show the world what her writing can truly do.

Here are some of Sophia's thoughts on the writing and revision of "Secret Star."

"Secret Star" is a beautiful poem in first-person narration. When you re-examined your verbs in your poem, did you see a difference in the tone of your poem? If so, what?

I found some changes. Sometimes, it does kind of change it.... because verbs absorb the reader into the poem. I felt like they let the reader be closer to the poem and gave a stronger feeling.

To revise your poem, what did you do? What was your process?

Before I revised anything, I looked through each comment and thought, "How could I change this?" I started at the top of the poem and went through each question. I went through it and through it, until it felt beautiful and it really absorbed what I was trying to do.

What was it like to have an editor read your poem? How did you feel about changing words or lines in your poem?

It was good to have someone be actually honest with me and give me good advice so it would be ready to publish. I didn't want to have a bad poem go out.

Secret Star

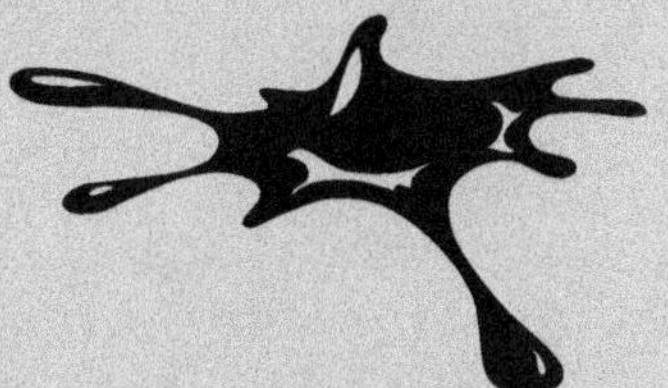

by

Sophia Calegari

344

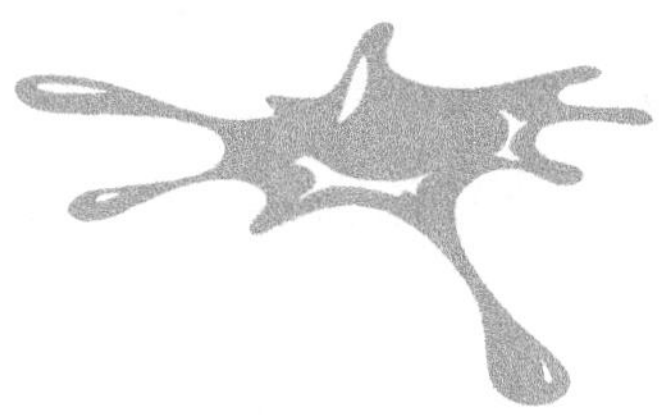

Luminous star

Shower a horizon of light

Wander

Through an arcing shadow

Create

The illumination of light

Walk to me

Walk to us

From the light

Of the cosmos

You feel your heartbeat

Come close

For let go of your secrets

And reveal your light

Brighten the moon

With your heavenly pearl

Don't reflect the lonely stars verbatim

Give the world

The beyond within you

You may hide your halo

From me

But all you need to seek

Is yourself

For this secret star

Is you

348

Similes & Metaphors

elinda Cordell mentored Adrien Villanueva through a revision focused on similes and metaphors in Adrien's poem, "If Noelle."

Dear Reader,

What's really cool about Adrien's poem is that it isn't saying, "Oh my sister is so perfect!" As anybody with sisters knows (I have two younger ones), sisters are definitely not perfect and sometimes they drive you just a little bit nuts, but you still love 'em. This poem does a great job of showing Adrien's relationship with her sister in a sweet and truthful way. Like the dog getting into her stuff but then bringing it back, and, like lemonade, her sister is sweet and sour at the same time. Those images make Noelle more human, more real. And since we like dogs and lemonade, the comparisons work nicely.

What is neat is that Adrien's comparisons are not actually metaphors. She's not saying "Noelle IS a drink of lemonade," she's saying, "IF she WERE a drink of lemonade, which she's not, but we're totally going to compare her to one," etc. That gives Adrien a little wiggle room to play with the image.

Similes and metaphors — comparisons — are fun to mess with. Similes, which use "like" or "as" in the comparison, give you that wiggle room. "My heart fluttered behind my ribs like a frightened bird." You aren't saying that your heart IS a frightened bird, but she sure feels like it. Metaphors, on the other hand, make a direct comparison and you have to be just about pitch perfect with them. "He filled the doorway, awkward as a horse" (novelist John Gardner wrote that line) turns a guy into a horse for the briefest instant, and a good metaphor really lights up the page. If you said, "He filled up the doorway, awkward as a bowling ball," the metaphor goes "thunk" and the reader thinks, "Bowling balls

aren't awkward!"

Here's an exercise to try: Write a poem that's a string of similes or metaphors. Think, "Well, maybe I want to compare my sister to an octopus," and then mess with that for a while. Sometimes you get really cool stuff when you try this. Sometimes you get really goofy stuff! That's exactly what you want! Be outlandish. Playing with words and images is a great way to sneak up on a poem when it's not looking.

I wrote a bunch of similes and metaphors into this letter without realizing it. How many can you find?

Write on,

Melinda

Melinda R. Cordell used to be a horticulturist but now works as a proofreader. She has three hens who follow her around the yard. She is currently working on a book about the Civil War as well as 20 other projects.

Adrien Villanueva

Special thanks to Noelle Villanueva, who wrote this bio for her sister.

Adrien, my little sister, was born on March 2, 2004. Adrien is a pretty nice and caring sister. Her grades in school are good, especially in math. Adrien and I play basketball with our Tatay (dad). I must say that she is a good shooter. At school she loves playing wall ball or chatting with her friends, though she talks too much in my opinion. This school year, Adrien performed in the variety show with her BFF Alyssa. Together they sang, Skater Boy, by Avril Lavigne. Even now she is already starting to plan for the next performance. Adrien laughs a lot, especially at my jokes! She also has a great imagination. When we were young we came up with stories our Barbies can star in. Her stories were especially crazy and dramatic. Adrien's favorite animals are horses and dogs. Adrien is very patient with our sweet, beautiful dog, Fauna, when she teaches Fauna new tricks. She's not as patient with me though! My sister is a very gifted writer and singer and I'm honored to be the subject of one of her poems.

Here are some of Adrien's thoughts on the writing and revision of "If Noelle."

What did you change when you revised?

I wrote a concluding stanza, and revised the 3rd line in my first stanza and the 3rd line in the 2nd stanza.

What advice do you have for Inklings in writing a poem?

I would suggest that if they wanted to write a poem, they should write about something they are interested in or something that inspires them.

Who do you like to share your poems with?

I like to share my poems with my family, and usually after I share them, I ask them on how I could make my poem better.

What do you like best about writing poetry?

What I like about writing poems is because it's fun to write them.

If you could be an animal, which one would you be, and why?

If I could be any animal, I would be a dog so that I can know what my dog, Fauna, is saying and so I can talk to her and she can talk to me too.

354

If Noelle

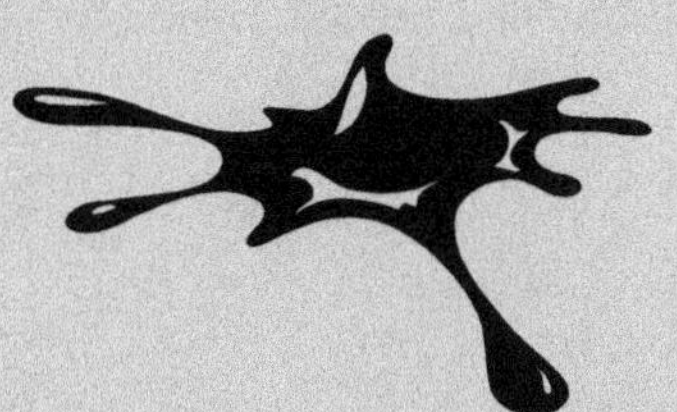

by
Adrien Villanueva

356

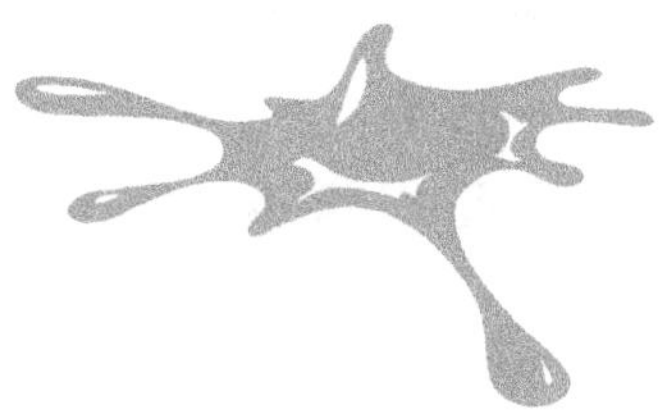

If Noelle was an animal
She would be a dog
Taking my stuff and hiding it well
Yet she always gives it back

If Noelle was a bird
She would be an owl
Although quite shy
She can be fierce too

If Noelle was a drink
She would be lemonade
Sweet and sour
At the same time

If Noelle was a color
She would be yellow
Always bright and cheerful

If Noelle was a fish,
A deer, or a bear
Whatever she is
She'll still be my sister.

Structure in Poetry

Jennifer Mazi mentored Elle Marsyla through a revision focused on structure in poetry for Elle's poem, "Circle."

Dear Reader,

In Elle Marsyla's "Circle," a free-verse poem about beginnings and ends, life and death, firsts and lasts, we chose to focus on structure, a revision choice inspired by Elle's question: does a poem have to rhyme?

The answer? No way.

A poem is a promise from the poet to the reader that every word, from the way it sounds to where it falls on the page, has been carefully considered. How a writer structure the words on the page gives power to the poem. Sometimes we find structure by playing with the way words look on the page, or through a certain format. In Elle's poem, notice three distinct chunks of words, or stanzas, chosen to signify a beginning, middle and end. Also notice the loop at the poem's end, which brings the reader back to the ideas presented at the beginning. The structure in this poem is a metaphor for life and its cycles.

A fun exercise to finding a structure in your free-verse poem is to consider removing all of the line spaces and punctuation marks. (AHH! I know!) Your poem will look like a jumbled paragraph. Go through and make BOLD the words or ideas that stand out to you the most.

Next, reposition the lines of your poem so the words in bold are at the end of each line. This may mean that the end of your sentence comes in the middle of a line. That's

okay! The reader's eye naturally lingers on the end of lines, so give that space to the most important, most exciting words within your free-verse poem, and watch a different structure gradually fall into place.

Write On,

Jennifer

Jennifer Mazi is a Writer of Many Things. She lives in Kansas City, MO, and is constantly on the prowl to find a Cloak of Invisibility. When she is not acting like a kid, she is making up stories for them, usually funny ones, sometimes involving talking planets.

Elle Marsyla

Elle is ten years old. She lives in Woodside, California and is inspired by nature because she is surrounded by trees. She has a younger sister named Pearl and an older brother named Holyfield, who is a cat. Her hobbies are writing, reading, soccer and running.

Here are some of Elle's thoughts on the writing and revision of "Circle."

Where did you get the idea for this poem?

> This poem came from thinking about death. I was worried about my cat dying, and so I was trying to turn death into a good thing, trying to convince myself that it wasn't that bad. After I thought it through, I noticed that it helps the environment because I'm nature crazy.

What did you have to think about when considering the structure of your poem during your revision?

> I had to think about making the lines shorter so that you slowed down to read it. A line doesn't have to be a sentence. And

poems don't have to rhyme or have any type of rhythm.

So you are the creator of your own page, and get to make up your own rules. How did that feel?

It's fun to do that because I don't like rhyming poems because you have to work too hard to find the right words that rhyme, but when you don't rhyme you can do anything you want.

What was the hardest part about your revision?

Making changes to it, because when it sounded right to me, I didn't want to change it, but when I did, I made it better. This process has taught me you have to really work to get things done, and to fit that work into your real life.

Circle

by

Elle Marsyla

366

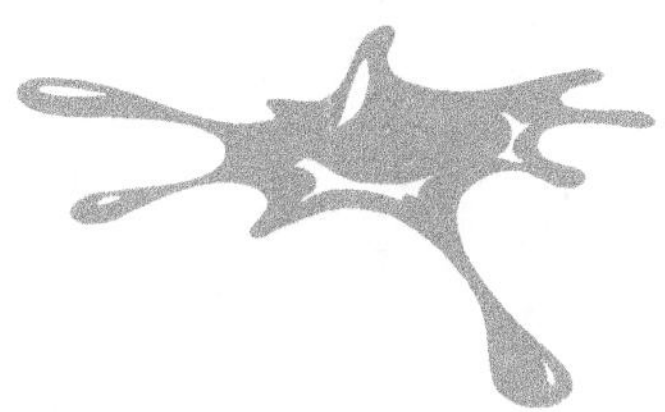

aindrops start at the oceans
where water turns into clouds
Clouds freeze and water comes down.
Slowly water turns into an ocean.
What comes first,
ocean or rain?

Rain falls as you are laid into the ground.
Small jewels sparkle
and create rainbows across our faces
Moss grows up the tall oak trees
casting a green glow.
Huckleberry weaves through a fence.
Two days ago I would have played

Circle

in the ferns next to me.
But I stare onward
and think.

Your life will never be lost.
Your body will turn into soil
and help trees grow.
The trees hold soil together
creating a nice path for a river.
The river will run to the ocean.
The ocean will turn into rain.
The rain will give life
What comes first,
life or death?

368

Mirror Poems

aomi Kinsman mentored Mickayla Blake through a revision focused on exploring poem's theme by creating a mirror poem for Mickayla's poem, "If It Were All Up to Me."

Dear Reader,

To me, poetry is one of the most difficult types of writing to revise. Poetry just IS. One has to understand the effect one seeks in order to address the question, "Is the poem working?"

In the best poems, the ones that come passionately from our hearts, sometimes stepping out of our own shoes and into those of the reader is more difficult still. When I read Mickayla's well-crafted, lovely poem, I didn't want to suggest a word change here or there.

Instead, I spoke with Mickayla about what the poem meant to her. I wanted to address theme, not because the poem couldn't stand alone as it was, but because in the conviction of her words I felt that Mickayla had even more to say on her subject.

So, instead of addressing her initial poem, we created a second poem, a mirror poem. Our aim was to make the abstract concrete in the second poem. I asked Mickayla: What might one specific hungry person look like, in your opinion? What would happen if that person were to be given food?

Using descriptive language, yet still working with poetic lines, we fleshed out scenes to make the concepts in Mickayla's original poem more tangible.

We agreed not to worry about how the poems would go together. Maybe they would blend into one poem, or maybe each would stand alone. Maybe the mirror poem would cause Mickayla to want to change a few things about their original poem. We didn't know.

In the end, the experiment was a success. Mickayla ended up with two poems that as a pair added levels and depth

to one another.

I encourage you to find ways to play with your work, particularly when you know there is more to be said on a subject. Theme is tricky. When one writes to a theme, sometimes the work comes out flat or preachy. For that reason, playing with form when thinking about theme is an excellent idea. Write a poem on your story's theme, for instance. Or write a journal entry on the topic of your poem to explore a concept. Deep thinking is part of being a writer, and often we need multiple windows through which to see clearly what we mean to say. I encourage you to be creative. Experiment. You never know what will come of your efforts.

Explore On,

Naomi

Naomi Kinsman is the author of *Spilled Ink, A Young Writer's Notebook,* and the *From Sadie's Sketchbook* series. One of her favorite parts about having founded Society of Young Inklings is meeting and working with so many talented young authors. She has an MFA in Writing for Children and Young Adults from Hamline University and lives in San Jose, CA.

Mickayla Blake

Mickayla is in seventh grade at Eastside College Preparatory School in East Palo Alto, California. She likes to read books and play volleyball. Her favorite book series is the *Divergent* series, and her favorite non-series book is *The Fault in Our Stars*. She wants to grow up to be a teacher, actress, or writer. Her favorite birds are the phoenix and the American eagle because they symbolize the success that she has had.

Here are some of Mickayla's thoughts on the writing and revision of "If It Were All Up to Me" and "A Change Made within Time."

What did you expect the revision process to be like?

I couldn't think of anything I'd want to change in my poem and so I thought it would be hard.

What did you think of creating a poem to mirror your original poem?

I liked the idea but I knew it would be hard to turn my poem into more of a specific story.

Was the process worth the effort?

It was because when I read it over, it goes with my first

poem. My new poem shows the first one as it if were in real life.

When you have a poem about big ideas, how do you come up with specific details the way you did for your mirror poem?

Read your first poem over and over. Imagine a character who fits and what they would actually do.

You ended up changing a few things about your original poem, too. You added a line and you created new line breaks. How did you come up with those ideas?

I added the question to the end of the original poem. It just happened that I was thinking of things that end with questions and I thought of that question to put on the end of my poem.

For my line breaks, I looked at the mirror poem and the line breaks we'd made there. Then, I tried to make line breaks in my original poem where they made sense.

Where is your favorite place to write?

My room because it is relaxing and comfortable.

You had challenges finding time to work on your writing. How did you solve them?

It's hard to get the time. I had to try to squeeze in time. With any free time you have, work on your writing and then when your schedule is more free, you can get into it. Any free time in a busy schedule is worth using to write, especially if you're as busy as I am.

What advice would you give to other poets?

Start by taking notes about whatever is on your mind, and from those notes you can create a poem.

If it Were All Up to Me & A Change Made within Time

by Mickayla Blake

376

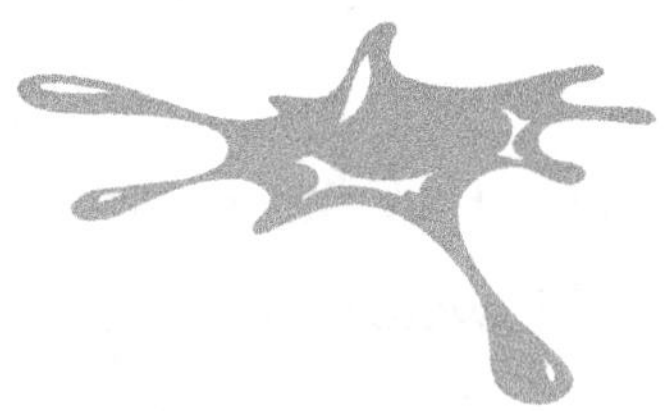

If it were all up to me
The poor would have riches
And the blind man would see

The hungry would eat
And the weak would be strong
And people with hatred would
All get along

The ones who are greedy would
Start to share
And unfriendly people would start to care

The thirsty would drink

And the deaf person hear
And sorrow and sadness
Would all disappear

And that is how the world would be
If it were all up to me
I finish with this question to you:
What would you do
If it were all up to you?

A man huddles on the city streets
Thin hair, old and grey
His cheeks hollow, his eyes pleading
His sign saying:
Looking for money,
Do anything for food

Then a young man comes along
In a coat and hat, very healthy looking
When he sees the old man
And reads the sign
He takes the man's hand

And brings him home

A few weeks later
The old man has a home
With a job and food to eat

He is now able to see clearly
And has a lot of strength
To go through the many challenges
That will come his way

He has no more hatred or greediness
He is full of kindness
And he puts other people's needs
In front of his own

There is no more sadness left in him
To get in his way
He will always remember
The young man
Who came when there
Was no more hope
And saved the day